THE BOOK OF CAIRO

First published in Great Britain in 2019 by Comma Press.
commapress.co.uk

'Gridlock' was first published in *Riham Photo Studio* by Dar al-Misriyya al-Lubnaniyya. 'Whine' was first published in *Biscuit and Molasses* by Dar al-Ain. 'The Soul at Rest' was first published in *Elegy* by Merit. 'Into Emptiness' was first published in *Negligence and Error* by Kotob Khan. 'The Other Balcony' was first published in *Death Wants me to Accept his Apology* by Dar al-Ain. 'Hamada al-Ginn' was first published online at www.wadita.net. 'Siniora' was first published in *The Case of the Murdered Mahragan Singer* by Merit. 'Two Sisters' was first published in *Rooms* by Kotob Khan. 'Talk' was first published in *Blink of the Eye* by Kotob Khan. 'An Alternative Guide to Getting Lost' was first published in *Churches Don't Fall in the War* by Misr al-Arabiyya.

A CIP catalogue record of this book is available from the British Library.
ISBN: 1910974250
ISBN-13: 978-1-91097-425-4

This book has been selected to receive financial assistance from English PEN's 'PEN Translates' programme.

The publisher gratefully acknowledges assistance from Arts Council England.

Printed and bound in England by Clays Ltd, Elcograf S.p.A

THE BOOK OF CAIRO

EDITED BY RAPH CORMACK

Contents

CONTENTS

Introduction

IF YOU GO TO CAIRO, whoever you are, you will find a thousand other people just like you. Or so a Mauritanian shop-keeper in New York once told me. I don't actually know if he had ever visited the city but, as for so many people, its sprawling diversity held an important place in his imagination. One of the biggest cities in Africa (*the* biggest by some estimations), this vast Nile-side people-magnet has played its part in more than its fair share of historical events. Among Cairo's patchwork geography, punctuated by the traces of the city's Pharaonic, Fatimid, Mamlouk, Ottoman, Khedivial, and Nasserist history, over 20 million people spend their lives.

The city's recent history has been no less eventful. In early 2011, protesters in Tunisia rose up against the 23-year rule of the president Zine el Abidine Ben Ali. People gathered in the street calling for him to leave chanting 'Bread, Water, No Ben Ali' and the now famous slogan 'The people want to bring down the regime'. On 14th January, Ben Ali left for Saudi Arabia. Tunisia provided the spark that ignited Egypt. On 25th January 2011, protesters gathered in Cairo's Tahrir Square calling for 'Bread, Freedom and Social Justice' and the fall of the regime. On 11th February, the people succeeded in bringing down Hosni Mubarak. Over the next two years, the city saw a succession of different leaders, organisations and political parties vying for power. From the Supreme Council of the Armed Forces to the

Muslim Brotherhood, alongside both a revolutionary front and the so-called 'remnants' of the Old Regime, competing interests struggled to win support. For many, it was a time of great hope and opportunity, for others, a period marked by uncertainty and dangerous instability.

All of that came to an end in the summer of 2013. The president Mohamed Morsi, affiliated to the Muslim Brotherhood, was forced from power and, after a sit in of several weeks, his supporters were violently expelled from Rabaa al-Adawiya Square. Many hundreds were killed.

Since then, the city has entered into a state of enforced forgetfulness. Those two and a half years, and their fatal conclusion, have been expunged from the public consciousness and many people are reluctant to relive them. Between 2013 and 2018, websites have been blocked, publishing houses have been raided, countless people have been arrested.[1] A giant Egyptian flag has been hung from a 20-metre pole erected at the centre of Tahrir Square.

One author featured in this collection, Ahmed Naji, published his dystopian novel, *Using Life*, in 2014. It tells the story of a decadent, crumbling city struggling to hold itself together – a nightmarish vision of Cairo's near future. The author was imprisoned in 2016, charged with obscenity after a reader who had read a serialisation of the novel in a literary journal said he suffered heart palpitations. The filth and decadence of Naji's vision of Cairo was too much for him.

Ahmed Naji's story in this collection, focuses on a sex-obsessed hashish cook, who lives in a dingy flat in Cairo which is only brightened by visits from his much more capable girlfriend. The writing is filled with a deep and varied sexual vocabulary, which has become one of Naji's trademarks, and a fascination with Cairo's underworld. It ends, with the disturbing air of prophecy, as the narrator prepares himself for jail.

This book tells the story of a city that is struggling to forget itself. As it goes to press, towering billboards on the major roads and bridges advertise apartments, villas or, merely, plots of land for sale in the desert compounds on the capital's outskirts. They have names like New Cairo City, Uptown Cairo, District Five, Hyde Park, and Mountain View and offer an escape from the oppressive crowds and traffic of the city. Even the government seems to be following the rush to the desert. They are now building a New Administrative Capital on Cairo's outskirts, which promises to take much of the bureaucratic work out of the centre and into an easily-manageable satellite.

In 2018 work started on a new project in the Maspero triangle, beside the Nile in the centre of the city. Bulldozers moved in and began to level this historic district, many of the crumbling houses in it having been declared unsafe. Nothing has yet risen to replace them but the plans show a project more influenced by recent developments in the Gulf than by the rest of the city.

In Tamer El Said's melancholic ode to Cairo, *In the Last Days of the City*, released in 2016, an image of sugar cubes dissolving in a cup of tea beside the protagonist's dying mother is juxtaposed with the demolition of a typical Cairene building. This same image of dissolving sugar, mirroring a dissolving city, is also used in Hassan Abdel Mawgoud's 'Into the Emptiness' included here. This short story highlights the confused narrator's growing disconnect from the world, which is, in turn, echoed by the barren, desert surroundings of his compound miles from the city. It is unclear whether his isolated life in this newly constructed urban experiment is driving him mad or it is, itself, a product of his madness.

For the visitor to Cairo, too, the experience of city has changed in much the same way. The Grand Egyptian Museum near the pyramids, has been designed to ensure that tourists do not have to brave the busy streets of downtown to see Egypt's ancient wonders; everything is grouped together on the Giza plateau and a sanitised experience of Cairo is all that is on offer to many travellers.

The ten stories in this collection, which were (with the exception of Nael Eltoukhy's prophetic 'Hamada al-Ginn') published between 2013 and 2018, capture the strange mood of post-Arab Spring Cairo, even if they are not explicitly political. They are dominated by forgetting, by a difficult relationship to reality and an uneasy retreat into the self. Eman Abdelrahim's dream-like and foreboding tale of narrowly avoided cannibalism and final escape into sleep, is a poetic example of a wider impulse. Areej Gamal's 'Alternative Guide to Getting Lost', with its ghostly bureaucrats and failed attempts at (literal) flight from Egypt, again captures the desire to escape that is so prevalent among young Egyptians (even if *what* they are escaping from, exactly, is often very different).

But the stories also feature the eccentrics, the romantics, and the tricksters who still populate the city's streets. Cairo is a city that has always felt on the verge of disintegration but, through it all, has always managed to hold at the centre. Perhaps this is thanks, in part, to the city's endlessly resilient sense of itself: a sense of self-possession or identity that beats like a pulse through all of these stories; it would take a brave gambler to bet on Cairo losing its vigour.

Since the early 20th century the short story has been one of the main genres to capture the everyday life of Egypt's residents. By the 1920s, the form had become a recognised and established genre, which frequently appeared in the pages of newspapers and literary journals. Writers were influenced especially by French and Russian traditions but, from very early on, there was always a strong drive to capture the lives and struggles of contemporary Egyptians in short fiction. It was said that whereas the novel was the genre of the rich, because novels had to be bought, short stories were for ordinary, poor Egyptians because they appeared on the pages of the newspapers that wrapped their daily falafel.

As the twentieth century progressed, Egyptian writers continued to hone their craft. The names Mahmoud Taymour and Youssef Idris stand out as pioneers, who each published several well-regarded collections of stories, but many other writers contributed to the genre's development over the 20th century (Ibrahim Aslan, Ihsan Kamal, Edward al-Kharrat, Naguib Mahfouz, etc.). In the early 21st century, almost every aspiring writer begins with a collection of stories; some use it as a stepping stone towards writing a novel and others become specialists of the form.

The short stories of the 2010s have come a long way from their century-old forbears. Writers have pushed the limits of style, form and content, often with bold experimentation. However, in many cases, the genre maintains its original mission to write about the experience of living in Egypt and its crowded capital city. The stories selected for this anthology offer exciting vignettes of life across Cairo – in its houses, in its offices, and on its streets.

The crowded streets and notorious traffic jams are playfully evoked in Mohamed Salah al-Azab's story 'Gridlock', as he weaves a web of different lives which come together on the busy 6th October Bridge. Hend Ja'far's 'Rest in Peace' brings us into the office of the obituary writer in the largest national newspaper, as a musician comes in to commemorate the death of a belly dancer. The reader is also taken inside Cairene houses in Nahla Karam's 'The Other Balcony'; its story of a love affair across a small alley is simultaneously a critique of the problems of gender in modern Egyptian relationships and a tale of an opportunity suddenly and inexplicably lost.

Even in difficult and uncertain times, it is possible to laugh and the famous Egyptian sense of humour infuses all the stories in this collection: from the biting irony of Nael Eltoukhy's imagined investigation to discover the whole truth of the universe, to the comically pathetic new Head of Department in Hatem Hafez's 'Whine'. The exchange between a disgraced doctor and the man whose job is to invent Cairo's rumours in Mohamed Kheir's 'Talk', is a small comic masterpiece.

Cairo today may be a city beset with difficulties and haunted by many ghosts. But there is still nowhere else quite like it in the world. It is also a city of great marvels, depth and vitality, which continues to produce astonishing literary talent. Independent publishing houses like Kotob Khan, Ain, and Merit (which, between them, first published most of the stories in this collection) continue to take chances with bold and experimental writing. Thanks to them, writers are still finding ways to give expression to the many different lives being lived in this already much-storied city, even as worries grow about direct and indirect censorship. Let these ten different stories, written by current and former residents of the city, be your introduction to its infinite variety.

Raph Cormack
Cairo, 2019

Notes

1. The latest news story, as this book goes to press, is that Khaled Lotfy, owner of Tanmia publishing house and bookshop has been sentenced to 5 years in prison for divulging military secrets after attempting to publish an Egyptian edition of the book *The Angel: The Egyptian Spy who Saved Israel*. An appeal may still be possible.

Gridlock

Mohamed Salah al-Azab

Translated by Adam Talib

THE MICROBUS ROLLS SLOWLY up the ramp to the October 6th flyover from Ahmad Abdel-Aziz Street right into heavy gridlock. A sheet of paper taped up in the rear window reads: 'For Sale (completely serious). '99 Kia w/ 2003 Toyota parts. License good for 1 more yr. Speak to Driver.'

The normal route that the microbus should have taken as it picked up and dropped off passengers began in Bulaq el-Dakrour, going down Sudan Street over to Arab League Street, then crossing May 15th Bridge to Esaf Square downtown – and then back again. But on his last circuit, the driver, Yasser 'the Dose', saw an upturned lorry at the edge of Sphinx Square, completely blocking his way back. He had uttered some choice words about the truck and its driver and then decided that he'd take Ahmed Abdel-Aziz Street to the October 6th flyover instead, and then try his luck at the Tahrir Square exit.

Yasser's breakfast spliff that morning was a dud. *Damn you, Nasser!* Nasser is the crook who sold him the half-finger of bogus hashish, which was mostly aspirin and henna. Now he has no choice but to confront him when he sees him tonight. He curses himself. He knows he should have spent that money on his baby daughter, Shahd. *I'll buy her some formula from the pharmacy before I go home tonight. Damn you, too, Safa!* His wife's chest dried up a mere month and a half after she'd given birth to Shahd.

Looking out across all the stationary cars around him, Yasser feels like he's in the middle of a giant car park. *Maybe I should have gone the normal way.* Shahd has just begun talking. 'Bama Baba'. He laughs to himself at the thought. Then, just as quickly, he frowns. He releases the handbrake: *Fuck this traffic! Fuck Sphinx Square, fuck the October Bridge, and fuck lorries especially! Fuck every single car out here!*

Alongside the microbus, a black Chevrolet Optra creeps up the ramp. Hussein, who likes people to call him 'The Engineer', bought it with a 60-month loan from NSG Bank which will end up costing him an additional 23,000 pounds in interest. The accountant at the bank had refused to write 'Engineer' under Hussein's title on the loan papers because he actually had a degree in law, not engineering. Hussein argued with him about the minimum mandatory insurance coverage; in the end he chose the most limited plan, which covered pretty much nothing. When his wife, Enas, tried to challenge him about it, he just kissed her on the cheek – that was his way of ending conversations. 'Have faith!' he said.

Hussein lives his life as though he really were an engineer. He even bought a hardhat, which he placed prominently in the rear window of his car, and he always tells the new people he meets to call him 'The Engineer'. His co-workers at Cleopatra Ceramics call him 'The Engineer' because he's a product designer.

Hussein didn't start driving the car as soon as he'd bought it; he took driving lessons first. He followed the advice of his co-worker Tamer, an actual engineer, and learned to drive a manual, even though he'd bought an automatic. If you learn to drive on a manual, Tamer explained, driving an automatic is like driving a bumper car.

Soon after he finished his driving lessons, Hussein discovered that driving the Optra wasn't nearly as easy as driving a bumper car. He drove it very carefully for a little while each day to prepare himself for the commute to work. Finally, he threw caution to the wind and started occasionally driving himself all the way to work even though he still didn't have a driving license. When Enas, told him he was being foolish, he gave her a light spank on the bum – which was his way of showing off – and said that his cousin was a police officer who could definitely help him out if he ever got into trouble.

Dressed in green overalls, Abdel-Rasul appears in the gap between the microbus and the Optra. He wiggles his broom from side to side to make it look like he's sweeping the tarmac. He looks directly at 'The Engineer', who looks everywhere except for into Abdel-Rasul's imploring eyes. All Abdel-Rasul can think about is how much it's going to cost him to marry off his daughter Asma. Asma's mother harangues him about it every day and Asma, for her part, tells her father that she is 'embarrassed to be the daughter of a street-sweeper'.

This brings us to Asma. She was supposed to have left the family home in Bulaq el-Dakrour this morning and walked down Nahya Street and then across the crowded pedestrian bridge to Sudan Street, where she would board the large 26-seater microbus that worked the Wooden Bridge to Giza route. The cost of a single journey had risen recently from 75 piastres to a pound and then from a pound to one pound 25, after a protracted dispute between passengers and drivers, which the drivers eventually won. She should have got up as the microbus turned by the Faculty of Fine Arts and said to the driver, 'Drop me at the main entrance, please.' Then, she should have alighted and gone on to campus to attend her public-sector accounting lecture, which she wouldn't have understood a word of. And then, exiting through the gate by the Faculty of Business, she should have gone to buy a study guide for 14 pounds. That was what she told her father she was going to do last night. He gave her 17 pounds: 14 pounds for the study guide, two and a half pounds for her bus fare, and 50 piastres for any incidental expenses.

But Asma didn't do any of that, except for the part about leaving her family home in Bulaq el-Dakrour and walking down Nahya Street. She went instead to meet Sherif, who worked at the mobile shop near her house. They'd got to know each other when she started going to the shop because, as she discovered, they didn't cheat you there on phone top-ups: when you gave them five pounds to top up your phone, you got a whole five pounds back in credit. The first few times she went to top up her credit, he'd ask her, 'What's the number, Beautiful?' and she'd smile despite herself and then he'd look at her and he'd smile too. After she'd gone to the shop a third time, he sent her a text message that read: 'This is just a little gift to say that you're sweet, Sweetie'. Her credit went up by five pounds.

Asma called Sherif at the shop to thank him for the five-pound top-up and they stayed on the phone until all five pounds ran out. When she tried to call him back, the automated voice on the other end said, 'I'm sorry, sir, but you don't have sufficient credit to make this call. Please purchase more credit and try again later'. BEEP. BEEP. BEEP.

Asma had gone to see Sherif at the shop this morning and when she'd arrived, she found him alone with another girl. She didn't know for certain whether she'd seen them kissing but she gaped at Sherif like a betrayed spouse and then turned and ran off. Sherif watched her leave, but he didn't go after her.

Before she knew it, Asma stood, crying, at the microbus stop. She ignored the rude comments directed at her by the driver's crew: one driver, and seven guys who were just hanging around him. Her phone rang. It was Sherif. She didn't answer until he'd called for a fifth time. When she told him where she was, he said he'd be there in a flash.

When Abdel-Rasul turns around, he spots a taxi driver with a big beard and mutters, 'God have mercy'. He hates anyone with a beard. This is almost entirely on account of his devout neighbour, Tareq, who nags Abdel-Rasul about changing his name whenever he bumps into him on the stairs. 'No one serves the Prophet without also serving God, so your name, Abdel-Rasul, Servant of the Prophet, is just plain blasphemy!' Abdel-Rasul doesn't like getting into arguments so all he ever does is shake his head and scurry off.

Hussein's wife calls and asks him to stop at Carrefour on his way home to pick up a value pack of Pampers (size 4) because their daughter has diarrhoea, and also to get some Persil (gel, not powder) because it's on offer and comes with an extra small bottle for free, as well as some Sensodyne toothpaste because all the other brands give you bad breath, oh and also, Roumi cheese, and lunch meat, and Dutch cheese, and cheddar, and pickles for sandwiches.

Hussein can't keep track of everything Enas is saying so he snaps at her and says he isn't a delivery service. Just send me a list on Whatsapp, he says.

Sherif held Asma's hand and swore that there was nothing going on between him and that girl she saw him with at the shop. When he suggested they go to the riverside together, she asked him, 'What about the shop?' He told her his brother was looking after it. Then he turned to ask a young driver standing nearby: 'Hey, mate, which microbus is leaving next?' That

5

'mate', who was none other than Yasser 'the Dose', pointed at his own microbus and Sherif and Asma climbed on board. 'The Dose' stared at Asma's ass. *Damn these big asses.*

Abdel-Rasul turns away from the bearded taxi driver and knocks on Hussein's window, pathetically raising his hand to his mouth, miming hunger. Hussein waves him away as Yasser watches.

Sherif and Asma are sitting in the back row beside an old lady, who is dozing, and three children. Sherif keeps trying to kiss Asma but she keeps stopping him. 'What about all these people?' she says. 'The hell with all these people.'

Abdel-Rasul gives up on Hussein and moves on to the next car, which is idling just parallel to where Asma and Sherif are sitting.

Enas' shopping list appears on Hussein's Whatsapp. The driver's assistant, who is sitting beside 'the Dose' nudges him: 'Things are heating up back there', he says, gesturing towards Sherif and Asma.

Sherif tries to kiss Asma.

Hussein reads the shopping list.

'The Dose' watches Sherif and Asma in the rear-view mirror as he lifts his foot off the brake and accelerates just the tiniest bit.

Abdel-Rasul stands on the other side of the window next to Asma as a driver hands him a pound coin.

'The Dose' rear-ends Hussein.

Hussein's mobile falls to the floor.

Abdel-Rasul turns to see what happened.

Sherif takes his lips off Asma's.

Abdel-Rasul and Asma lock eyes. She sees him begging in the street, he sees her in Sherif's embrace.

'The Dose' and Hussein both leap out of their vehicles.

Let the battle begin.

Talk

Mohammed Kheir

Translated by Kareem James Abu-Zeid

I WAS BESET ON all sides by the rumours. It wasn't long after seeing my name in that newspaper article – 'Doctor Forgets Surgical Scissors in Patient's Stomach' – that I was clearing out my clinic. I kept telling people I wasn't even a surgeon, that I never performed any operations, and that the newspaper article was a big mistake. None of it did any good. Even after I published a lengthy rebuttal in the same paper, allegations on the internet continued to surface, claiming I had been 'referred for investigation' and had been 'barred from working.' 'Murderous Surgeon Still Receiving Patients: Where's the Doctors' Union?' ran another angry headline, contradicting the online rumours. Between one newspaper article and another, I read several extremely arrogant and ignorant replies – somehow written under my own name – to the newspaper's questions. No one had ever asked me those questions, but my supposed replies further incensed the reading public, and people began asking themselves: 'Who will protect us?'

Before long, this nightmare relocated entirely into the realm of reality; I found myself sitting on the floor of my clinic and staring at the gathering dust, which was now empty even of footprints.

Then Hasna suddenly cut ties with me. At first, I thought she was simply walking out on me because times had become

7

hard, but one day she fell apart in our bedroom. She confronted me with 'the truth' and passed judgement on me, claiming there must be a woman who was 'taking revenge on me by spreading the rumours.' She made me listen as she read out the emails and letters she had 'patiently endured' over the past few weeks, which had come to her from everywhere, warning her about me and revealing how I was 'deceiving' her. She felt she was in danger, and I was too shocked in that moment to find an appropriate response. In any man's pleading, innocence and guilt are one and the same, since both the innocent and the guilty issue the same denials.

This is how my home, following my clinic's lead, came to be empty too. I made desperate attempts to restore my reputation. I now knew how it felt to be scorned by everyone, even the doorman to my own building. Those suicidal thoughts I had said goodbye to after my teenage years awoke in me once more, and, at night, as I paced between the living room and the balcony, I began to ask myself: if I jump, should I do it wearing my pyjamas, or should I dress for the occasion? Should I do it with eyes open or closed?

Some time after this, I woke up one afternoon beside an almost empty bottle. I was about to polish it off, but I saw that evening was coming back around quickly, and that things were about to repeat themselves. So I resolved to break the cycle. I started leaving the house again and walked to far-off neighbourhoods where no one knew who I was. To tell the truth, I usually made my way to the bars in those neighbourhoods, to sit in a corner and look at the other lonely faces. I never tried to imagine the stories behind those faces. I just stared at them with nothing but hatred in my heart.

One of those nights, an old friend of mine called Hussein came and sat down near me. At first, I didn't recognise him, nor he me, but we gradually became aware of one another and started talking. It was a pretty incoherent conversation, but as the night and the wine wore on, he suddenly began to cry. He said his conscience couldn't bear it anymore. He borrowed a pen from the waiter and wrote a name on one of the napkins on our table, which he proceeded to hand to me: 'This man's behind everything that's happened to you.'

I stared at the name in surprise. I wasn't familiar with it. 'Is he a doctor too?' I asked Hussein.

'No, an architect,' Hussein replied, before leaving me in a state of shock.

I gave them a fake name when I called. And when my appointment came round, I headed over to his office, hoping to enter the building one man and leave another. I hesitated at the door to the ornate architecture consultancy office and read the name of its owner – the same name Hussein had written down on the napkin. I ran over the various scenarios I had prepared in my mind that would help broach the matter at hand, but the prospect of the whole story amounting to no more than the ravings of a drunkard cast a long shadow. In the end I told myself to simply go in, let the cards fall where they may. The only thing I had to lose was my despair.

A young woman led me inside. As I followed her down the corridor, I noticed how gracefully she walked – it reminded me of Hasna. I shook my head, took a deep breath, and entered the large office she had brought me to. I was received at the door by a man of medium height with a huge stomach. He was wearing a full suit and a welcoming smile that faded as soon my face came into the light. He looked at me for a moment before taking a seat behind his desk. The secretary closed the door, and I sat down in turn, my heartbeat quickening.

He studied a piece of paper in front of him and read the fake name I had given the secretary, then looked up at me and smiled: 'Welcome, Doctor. Why this deception?'

I did not reply; all the scenarios I had imagined evaporated. The architect continued, 'I suppose, then, we could say that this appointment is also fake. Doesn't that seem like a fair conclusion?'

I maintained my silence, so he went on: 'Who sent you? Never mind, it's not important. I hope you're not taking the whole thing personally. You don't know me, and I didn't know you either. I was just doing my job, nothing more.'

I stared at the elegant desk: 'Your job?'

He stared at the desk in turn, as if he were as surprised as I was: 'This? No, Doctor, I'm talking about what brought you here. It's very regrettable, it's a real shame, Doctor, I swear. As for this office – and the secretary, the sketches, the designs – it's all a show, a cover, you could even call it a 'rumour.' You've had some experience with rumours lately, haven't you? Sorry, I'm very sorry, that's flippant of me. Please accept my apology.'

'You're not an architect then?' I asked, utterly lost.

He responded with displeasure: 'Of course I'm an architect. What kind of person do you take me for, Doctor? An idiot? A freeloader? A fake? I have a talent. Don't you have a talent? Or some hobbies? Of course you do – all doctors have a talent. Do you write literature – poetry, perhaps? Do you paint?'

'I've got some talent. Or rather, I used to have some. And you? What's your talent? Destroying reputations?'

He shook his head so forcefully that the whole of his massive stomach quivered along with it: 'No, Doctor, please, that's a shameful misrepresentation. But you haven't had anything to drink. That's not right, it's just not right – what are you drinking?'

I had imagined that, within the first few minutes of entering the place, I would have my hands around the man's neck, but the dizziness that crept over me led me to respond in the same simple way: 'Coffee with sugar.'

He laughed as he got up: 'Coffee? *Coffee?*'

He pulled aside a curtain in the corner of the room, revealing a full bar – not a wine closet, mind you, but a real bar, albeit a small one, with a table and chairs and a sofa. He turned on the light and stood there, welcoming me like a dear friend: 'Please, Doctor, come on in.'

I followed him, and he pulled aside another curtain – this one in front of a window – so we could look out on Cairo at night. We sat down at the table and he poured two glasses of something he said he could 'personally vouch for.' He handed me my glass while I observed the delicate grace of his movements, which belied his size. He pointed out the window: 'What do you think of the view? Wonderful, isn't it? What were we saying? Oh yes, we were saying that that's a shameful misrepresentation, quite offensive. Destroying reputations, Doctor? That's an insult. An insult I'm willing to overlook, since you're my guest.'

I held my rage in check, which didn't require much effort, since my bewilderment and my despair – together with the glass in my hand – were having a pacifying effect on me: 'Excuse me, but I believe my reputation *was* destroyed. I think's that's precisely what happened to me. There's no other name for it. It's not a misrepresentation at all.'

He leaned forward and replied in a strange tone, as if it to reproach me: 'But doctor, haven't you ever made any mistakes? What's the difference between (and here he made quotation marks with his fingers) 'Scissors Forgotten in Patient's Stomach' and… Before I continue, I should say I know you're not a surgeon. Still, haven't you ever made a mistake? Haven't you ever diagnosed something as a simple stomach ache, for example, when it turned out to be much more serious?'

A distant memory arose in my mind, but I quickly stifled it and said: 'Everyone makes mistakes.'

'True,' he said, as if he had expected my reply, 'but no one admits them, especially not when they forget something as obvious as that, a simple diagnosis. You could have saved the poor old woman, no? Common gallstones – a reasonable diagnosis. An intelligent doctor such as yourself couldn't spot that?! You just let it be, just let it wreck her bowels? May God have mercy on everyone, and on the times when public hospitals were still the norm.'

The pain of the memory came back fiercely, and I started to ask him: 'Are you...'

He cut me off, laughing: 'No, no, I'm not the woman's son or anything like that. This isn't some Egyptian movie. We learned about the incident through routine research.'

He winked at me: 'Rest assured, your secret's safe.'

I slammed the glass on the table: 'Secret? You've disgraced me with your rumours.'

He lifted his finger: 'But they're false, Doctor, they're only lies. They'll run their course in due time. What would hurt you more? Lies, or the truth?'

I stared at him in silence, the strange trace of a smile still on his face. He continued: 'At least you can deny lies honestly, with a clear heart. You can face their cruelty with the indignation of someone who's being oppressed. People respond to the cries of the oppressed – isn't that right, Doctor?'

'Yes, by God,' I replied with irritable sarcasm.

He laughed: 'Don't invoke God against us.'

Becoming more animated, I said: 'Who are you, then? A secret organisation that takes revenge on doctors' pasts?'

He suddenly wore an annoyed expression on his face: 'Don't make fun of me, Doctor, and don't think I'm seeking revenge. I receive an assignment and I do my job. Business is business, as they say.'

I opened my mouth, but he beat me to it: 'Don't ask me

who I work for. It would be better if you asked *yourself* some questions instead. Another glass?'

He got up and moved with the same delicate grace, then suddenly stopped in his tracks to put another question to me: 'Do you remember Salim al-Ghayati?'

The question caught me off guard. 'The politician?' I asked cautiously.

'Mmm hmm.'

'Isn't he the one whose son died of a heroin overdose, in that dancer's apartment?'

He looked at me and smiled: 'More or less.'

He pointed at his chest with something resembling pride: 'The son died in an accident at home – he fell and smashed his head. The dancer owned an apartment in the same building. The heroin was one of the father's habits. I flipped everything around, and now, after all these years, I see it as a kind of archetypal rumour. You could say that many people have replicated it. But it was the first of my successes, and it introduced me to the world of politicians.'

'But the son...' I started, shocked.

He interrupted me: 'He's in the Hereafter, and none of our talk can harm him there. But our words struck down his father. Do you play pool?'

I shook my head, but I imagined al-Ghayati in the form of a billiard ball on a green table.

'People believed the story about his son, which was very damaging to him. But before all of that happened, they had failed to believe any of al-Ghayati's *actual* transgressions because they weren't titillating enough.'

He sat down again and continued: 'I'm not performing some kind of social role, nor am I taking revenge on anyone. I'm just doing my job. Don't think it's easy. The kids on the internet spoil my work, they make up all kinds of nonsense, stupid lies they call rumours. Distinguishing the authentic rumour from the forgery is becoming more difficult every day, I don't deny that. The whole country is going that way – cultural decay.'

I couldn't stop myself from laughing.

He looked at me and smiled: 'What? Doesn't the author of the rumours have the right to complain?'

'The 'fabricator' of the rumours, you mean.'

'What's the difference?'

I couldn't find one, so I said: 'Maybe I just don't believe it's a profession.'

'Then you think all those rumours sprouted up out of thin air? You think all the competing companies and security apparatuses don't need artists and curators?'

I started laughing again.

He gave me a defiant look, and spoke slowly: 'Why do you think I did research on your past, then? Do you take me for some lawyer looking for chinks in your armour?'

He raised his hands, as if to make a shape of some sort, and looked between them: 'The true rumour, if I may be permitted the expression, must resemble its target, must touch something within that target.'

The old woman I'd killed through neglect in my early years popped into my head again. I gulped down my drink and listened as he continued: 'A rumour is only complete if there's a reaction. So I ask you, my dear respected doctor: Why'd you start making the rounds of cheap bars? Why'd you start acting like you were guilty?'

I knocked my empty glass down on the table, but he didn't offer to fill it again. His voice, however, suddenly regained its cheerfulness: 'But here I am telling you the secrets of the trade for free. At your service, Doctor. It's because I don't usually meet the subjects of my work.'

'The *victims* of your work.'

'There are no victims over the age of thirty, Doctor. You're still alive at least, aren't you?'

'More or less.'

'Don't be a pessimist. You've got your whole life ahead of you, and life's cruel to everyone. Do you think I started out like this? I had my ambitions too. Didn't I ask you about hobbies? I used to write stories that no one ever read. But I was only successful at rumours. I'll remain an uncredited author, but at least I'll be a well-off one. And who knows, maybe one day I'll achieve some immortality.'

I repeated the word under my breath: 'Immortality.'

He corrected himself: 'Immortality within our profession, of course: a respectable conspiracy theory, one that stands the test of time. Isn't that right?'

He smiled and looked at his watch: 'I'm truly happy to have seen you.'

I suddenly roused myself: 'You're not going to tell me who...?'

He cut me off, as usual, and said in a tone that seemed to express disappointment: 'You just don't get it. You haven't seen the truth, Doctor, have you? Your enemy is no longer your enemy. Your enemy *now* is talk, opinions, impressions.'

'The rumour mill,' I said.

'The rumour mill,' he repeated, nodding his head.

I got up, but stayed standing where I was: 'I'm not leaving until…'

I fell silent. Until what? I didn't know.

But he nodded, a warm smile on his face, and said, 'Fortunately, I believe in specialisation.'

He led me back to his desk where, just for a moment, I was blinded by the light. I watched as he wrote something on a piece of paper. 'This is the number of someone who specialises in dispelling rumours. Tell them I referred you.' Then he laughed, 'But I doubt they're offering any discounts.'

I stared at the piece of paper. He'd also written down the name of a woman. 'She's the owner of a beauty salon,' he said.

'Call and make an appointment. I don't think it's far from your place.'

He suddenly reached his hand out to my stubbled chin: 'They'll take care of you – on both counts.'

The beautiful young woman led me outside. As I was leaving the building, I realised I hadn't asked how much it would cost. Then it occurred to me that running into Hussein at the bar might not have been a coincidence. I stood there in the cold night and stared at the piece of paper – at the phone number and at the woman's name – and I thought of Hasna once more, and hesitated a moment. Then I remembered my empty home, and made up my mind. I called the number and got the address, resolved to head over there without delay.

Whine

Hatem Hafez

Translated by Raphael Cohen

ONLY A FEW WEEKS since being made Head of Department, and already he realised he was missing the warmth afforded by a large shared office teeming with government employees, all making their amiable commotion. He smiled as he remembered the electric kettle with its peculiar high-pitched whine that provided the material for so many jokes and sarcastic asides, especially when Mr. Kamel – an excellent impersonator of his superiors – did his exaggerated impression of the former Head of Department's voice in the style of said kettle coming to boil. The memory made him wonder whether Kamel was still in the habit of brazenly mimicking his superiors and go on to wonder if he too should start to feel persecuted. Was Kamel making *his* voice sound like the whine of the kettle right now, given that he was Head of Department? The idea stung him in a sensitive spot, and, all of a sudden, he leapt up and flung open the door to his large office.

He should have been able to hear the voices of the staff in the shared office opposite that housed Kamel and his old colleagues, but a glass partition between the rooms intervened and stopped any sound from reaching him. He could see the staff laughing noiselessly – proof that the glass partition was in league with them, conspiring to stop him discovering the terrible extent of their mockery. But on the way back to his plush, comfortable seat, he convinced himself that Kamel could not possibly be making fun of him. They were friends, at the very least, and had often spent many hours in the café after work playing backgammon.

Now, though, and now in particular, he was coming to realise how lonely he was in his large office with its unnecessarily large desk. He also remembered that he could not pinpoint the last time he had met Kamel at the café. The duties of his new post and his efforts to consolidate his position with the Chairman of the Board had meant that he didn't have time to meet with his old friend. He wiped his glasses and tried to reassure himself that this was not a sufficient justification for Kamel to make fun of him, certainly not enough to turn his voice into the irritating metallic drone of the electric kettle.

He went back and shut the door. When he was satisfied that nobody could hear him, he started uttering nonsensical disjointed sounds and phrases. Then he began to sing in a loud voice, reassuring himself that his voice did not sound like the whine, any whine. But his loneliness only grew worse. He could feel his own self-pity growing alongside the crushing loneliness that was starting to make the walls of the large room close in around him – the room that was his and his alone.

He contemplated the office as if seeing it for the first time, as if he had just woken up from a deep sleep and found himself there alone. He saw his desk stretching so far in front of him that even if he extended his arms as far as they went, he could not reach the edges. He was sometimes forced to stand just to reposition the desk clock or take a pen from the penholder.

The arrangement of the objects on his desk was disconcerting, so he shifted everything around to move it within reach: the clock, the penholder, the calendar, the letter opener, paper, folders. But in the end that did not satisfy him either. The desk looked ridiculous, its vast surface bare as the desert with a pile of things stuck in one corner, no use to anyone. The desk was now an empty pedestal, its colossal size superfluous to requirements and its polished surface irritating.

He put everything back the way it had been and decided that it must be the desk's position in the room that was the problem; it was far from convenient. He summoned the two teaboys to come and move the desk and rearrange his unnecessarily spacious room.

He stood like an idiot in the centre of his room for a few moments not knowing what he wanted exactly and feeling a complete fool. A task of immense moment had suddenly befallen him. It was true that the furniture comprised no more than a desk, a small filing cabinet, and a small bookcase filled with books belonging to the ex-Head of Department. Yet it seemed as if he was on the verge of rearranging the whole world; he had never previously contemplated any undertaking on this scale.

Eventually, he settled on the idea of first moving the desk into a position opposite the door so that he would be able to observe his staff in the room that faced his. The door and the glass partition would block out the sound of their conversations and the jokes they cracked every now and again, but he thought it would at least allow him to keep an eye on Kamel, whose desk would be in full view all the time. Plus, with a little work on his lipreading, he would finally and permanently be able to divine all the little secrets they were hiding. He thought about all his plans as he went along the corridor that separated his office from the other employees' room, who seemed more malicious than he had suspected in all the years he had been one of them.

As he passed by, he noticed that the staff were sneaking glances at him – since his promotion it was unusual to see him loitering in the corridor, peering through the glass like someone window-shopping on a deserted street. He tried very hard to make his loitering appear natural and took great care that no one should notice that he was spying on them, yet those few brief moments of curiosity were enough to expose him. Just realising that they had begun to look at him was enough to make him feel naked. To make matters worse, he caught a glimpse of them laughing – in his view, hysterically and malignly – and, of course, Kamel was in the middle of it all, standing there, his fat body quivering as he impersonated who knows who. The whole scene was quite simply beyond bearing. He felt his face flush red with indecent speed. He hadn't blushed like this since becoming the fear-inducing Head of Department. He recalled how his face used to suddenly flush red whenever he was called in by the former Head of Department – the one whose voice sounded like a metallic whine – before he retired. For years he had fought to stop it happening or at least conceal it from his superior. He considered returning to his office and summoning Kamel, wondering if the man's face would also flush red or whether he had more control over it. He would have given his right arm to see that.

He went back to his office, not to summon Kamel – the very idea made him ashamed of himself – but to inspect his rearranged room. He sat down on his plush, comfortable chair and felt relaxed, content with its new location. A strange happiness came over him, the likes of which he had not felt for years. A happiness of unknown origins; it was not due to his promotion, of course, or the fact that he was sitting in his own office, or that he was relaxing in a chair with castors that meant he could swivel around without difficulty. He was confident that his happiness had no connection to any of those things. Even though the moment when his eyes had met Kamel's – as he stared ahead through the door and the glass partition – almost destroyed that happiness, he still clung onto this overwhelming feeling of joy that had come to him at the end of a lifetime. It had more strength in it than is contained in any look exchanged between two men. A glass of mint tea right then, he thought, would be an appropriate reward for such tenacious insistence on his own happiness.

He stretched out an arm to call the teaboy for a glass of mint tea but discovered that, since he had moved his desk, calling the teaboy was no longer possible. The push button was fixed to the wall next to where the desk used to be. Now that he had moved the desk, there were only three ways to call the teaboy: to get up – every time – and press the button on the opposite wall, which was hardly practical; or to get up – again every time – and go out of his office to call him in, which was surely a waste of time; or to leave his door permanently open so as to be able to call in him whenever he wanted. This last option seemed embarrassing, even humiliating, and not at all in keeping with his own value. For what if the teaboy did not hear him? Then he would be obliged to shout. And what if the teaboy pretended not to hear his raised voice and ignored him? Hadn't he done exactly the same with the former Head of Department when he had been tired out from running errands?

He felt the world was conspiring to destroy his happiness, but his remaining determination to cling on to it forced him to think quickly; he came up with an idea to demand that the push button be moved next to his desk. This solution was a stroke of genius, the product of a moment's inspiration. No, it was more than that; he took it as a sign of his innate superiority that had been summoned forth by the exigencies of his new position. He was the right man in the right place.

However, it was only a few short moments before he was saying to himself, 'It looks like today isn't my lucky day.' For, just as he was about to give the order to move the push button closer to his new position, it became obvious that his original idea of moving the desk from its old spot had not been a very good idea at all. One look around the place after its rearrangement was enough to vindicate such a belief. He discovered, for instance, that the bookcase, in its old position, played the role of someone harbouring a hardened criminal: it concealed behind it part of the wall, specifically the rot-eaten part. Even after he had gotten over his initial shock at the sight, he could not work out if the wall had taken advantage of his negligence – and the former Head of Department's negligence – and grown rotten over time, or had always been so. Had its crime occurred recently and remained undiscovered because it was a section covered by a bookcase, not needed by anyone? Or, had the bookcase, in fact, been intentionally placed in front of that spot to hide the severe distress to the wall? Or, indeed, had that section of wall decided to punish *him* for the neglect it had suffered over the course of many years at the hands of successive Heads of Department?

Although this last notion should have been dismissed outright as irrational fantasy, the obsessive doubts that had begun to assail him made him think it could be a strong possibility; in fact, there was considerable evidence that seemed to support such a view. Here was the filing cabinet, stuck against the wall dividing the room from the bathroom and, hiding behind it, another bloom of damp had started to exude the smell of mould. Here was the desk, like the Sphinx standing guard over the Necropolis, over an area of carpet the same length and breadth as the desk that seemed to have been meticulously and expertly flayed. It was not just a different colour, but had turned colourless. Of course, it was true that the room's carpet did not resemble any normal carpet in the slightest, but it did at least make the floor of his office feel like the floor of other Departmental Heads' offices in other government departments.

The way things were turning out depressed him. He felt a black sadness take root in his mind that he feared would stay forever. His suspicions had spread too far; it wasn't just people: at that moment he knew there must be a hidden power somehow manipulating his entire fate. If it hadn't been for his natural composure, he would have burst into tears right then and collapsed into his plush, comfortable chair, which he was no longer so sure befitted his position. He tried to remember when, in his time at the department, the room had been arranged differently. Going over the sequence of memories he had on this question made him rule out the effects of any hidden power. He replayed his memories of the room and, despite the changes in its occupant over the course of more than a quarter of a century, he could not think of a single occasion when it had looked different. At that point, naturally, he felt that rearranging the room had been an unnecessary folly. He therefore told himself that it was for the best that things returned to their time-honoured configuration, and that nothing in the whole wide world was more beautiful than things' being where they always had been. He felt a surge of joy and exaltation as he ordered the teaboys to restore the room to its original arrangement, ignoring their puzzled and suspicious looks.

While the teaboys put the things back to the way they had been prior to his sudden caprice, he left the room feeling extremely pleased with himself. Going suddenly out into the corridor separating his room from the employees' shared one had a startling effect, akin to pressing freeze-frame. The staff had, as was usual in the absence of a supervisor, been shouting at each other. It was not difficult to imagine what they might have been shouting about, and, from his experience with them as a former colleague, he started to come up with possible causes. They only ever got agitated about a small number of things, but these tiny things occupied the vast majority of the staff's time. They burst out laughing and shouting or caused some giant commotion without seeming to care why. As soon as he had become an onlooker outside the room – an onlooker spying through the glass partition – he had discovered that there were really not many reasons at all. What few there were basically concerned the whine of the electric kettle that worked infrequently but more frequently not at all. His proof of this theory was that as soon as he went into the corridor, the staff stopped their shouting. Kamel was standing in the middle of the room holding the kettle, whose whine sounded like... Well, were it not for the glass partition, he would have been able to hear.

Like a stone hitting a pane of glass, his spirits shattered onto the faded tiles of the corridor. Why had the staff stopped shouting as soon as he appeared? Why was Kamel holding the kettle in his long hands like an actor alone on stage? Why was there that look of panic on his face? Did their shouts have something to do with the kettle and its whine, or was it a ludicrous and unlucky coincidence (not that his luck had been good up to now)? He considered immediately summoning Kamel and warning him about the damage that his unruliness was causing among the staff. He also contemplated giving him a choice between the staff or the kettle. In the end, however, he was content to gather up his spirits from the corridor floor and put off any argument he might be forced into, especially at the beginning of his tenure in office. Nevertheless, he decided at very least he would not withdraw from the battlefield, but remained standing in front of everybody giving a look of defiance through the glass partition – a look for which he almost envied himself. Only a few moments later, the heartbeat returned to the room, not the lively heartbeat of just before, but a weak pulse that was enough to keep it and the staff alive. Seeing Kamel return to his desk like an actor being booed off the stage, he felt he had achieved a crushing victory in his first sortie as the new Head of Department.

He went back to his room swelling with pride at this great triumph, enjoying the stillness of his staff in their room. It made him feel just how much they feared him, which itself gave him the sense that things in that room had gone back to the way they were before. His desk was back in its old spot and the faded patch of carpet was no longer visible. He felt that all the bad things he had done in the past and all the crimes he would ever commit in the future were precisely concealed under the weight of that long, wide desk. He regained his calm and self-confidence when he sat down on the plush, comfortable chair and was reassured to find the push button within reach. Now, he could summon the teaboy whenever he wished, and, through him, he could also summon whomever he wished from the staff and address them from where he sat in his plush, comfortable chair protected behind the large desk. Now, for the first time, he sensed the beauty and grandeur of the office. He felt that he had not yet had the time to develop a proper appreciation of that office, and that he might need more time to understand that his presence in that room was the most important event to have happened to him in his entire life.

He did not, however, lack the time to understand how important it was for him to be in that room as Head of Department – even more, how important it was to be, for the moment, whether it be long or short, the *new* Head of Department. He thought about dying his hair as soon as he got home; looking like an old man might suggest that he was getting ready for retirement and, if he was treated on that premise, he would lose half his prestige. Looking young would preserve his image as the *new* Head of Department, and make everyone think that many years would have to pass before he became an *old* Head of Department.

Those who knew him well would swear that this was the fastest decision he had ever taken in his entire personal or professional life, a calm life otherwise devoid of snap decisions. Only a few seconds further and he was taking the second quickest decision of his life. He relaxed in his plush, comfortable chair and pressed the push button. When the teaboy came in, he told him, while shuffling a file in front of him to give the impression that what he was about to say was of no importance: 'Tell Mr. Kamel to come in,' before adding with confidence, 'Quickly!'

The Soul at Rest

Hend Ja'far

Translated by Basma Ghalayini

I work at *Al-Ahram*; you know it, that venerable daily newspaper established by the Lebanese gentleman. I can't recall his name, was it Niqula or Bishara!? Something like that, I don't remember exactly, and I can't be bothered to move from my seat to go through a pile of newspapers to check. Perhaps there were two founders? Or one? I don't know and, to be honest, I don't want to.

What I want to say won't take more than a page, maybe two. But one thing is for sure, regardless of the number of pages, it won't make a difference to anyone but me. I just want to vent so *I* can feel better about what I'm going through.

Like most of the writers in this part of the world, I am from the countryside: rural folk have a story worth telling, it seems. People from the city haven't gone through the same hardships as us. I was hoping that my story would start the way they all do: an absent father who only left behind a couple of carats of land;[1] a mother who raised her children without ever expecting help or compensation from them for all her years of toil and deprivation, before eventually falling ill and passing away – the usual backstory. But no, my story is a little different: my father died aged 45, from hepatitis. He passed away in an open ward beside 12 other patients at the University Hospital.

During the final days we spent with my father, or rather with his corpse in the early stages of decomposition, his stomach swelled up so much that it looked like it was about to explode. We never knew what our father did for a living exactly, just like the rest of the men in the village. The only thing different about him was that he didn't live long enough to buy his own land. He spent his life working as a tenant farmer for a landlord. Nonetheless, our needs were always met and we were never deprived of anything.

My mother didn't change with the death of my father, she still sells milk and cheese in the *bandar*.[2] She wakes up early for the *Fajr* prayer,[3] then takes the train to our regional capital, which takes thirty minutes. After she arrives she sets up in front of the main mosque and the customers come flocking to her. She is always sold out by the time of *Dhuhr* prayer.[4] Her secret, she says, comes from what she calls her sweet words and, 'People like to hear sweet words,' she would say. Thursday and Friday would always be her days off when she would cook aged rice along with a bird, slaughtered the same day. When we were younger, we all used to gather around the food; sometimes we would stay up roasting corn, or peanuts, until one of us fell asleep, at which point my mother would announce that it was time for bed.

My mother still works with the same energy, even though she now works two instead of five days a week.

She had a routine. She would come back home in the afternoon, have a small bite, and then start preparing for the following day. She would line up the cheese pieces, fill plastic bottles with milk, and set aside some goats' cheese for one of her customers, who was ill. She would also make sure to prepare the *mish*[5] which always sold out first, and never forgot to put out a bunch of rocket and other vegetables with the rest of her products before performing the *Isha'* prayer[6] and going to bed early, only to start the whole thing over again the next day.

When I started working in Cairo, every time I went to visit her I would come back laden with her goods. My colleagues would compete with each other to buy them off me, with the proceeds going back to my mother the next time I visited. She would laugh and say, 'This is your *Eideya*, Mohammad.'[7] I would kiss her hand, place the money in her lap, and top it up with what I could from my salary.

So why this long introduction? I don't know!

Did I mention that I work on the obituaries pages? It is what I have done since I first set foot in this revered institution that lies sleeping on one side Al-Gala'a Street. According to my colleagues, I work in the most read section of the newspaper. My job is to provide the customers with quotes for the notices they want to place, based on the position, size and day of the obituary. Friday's price, for example, is different to the rest the week; a right-hand page has a different price to the left. Placing an obituary on the right side of a page is different to placing it on the left side; and the price also differs depending on whether you want to place it at the top or the bottom of the page. Each has a different price; the customer can decide.

I have come across all kinds of ways to dishonour the dead. One day a woman in her early forties visited us to request an obituary for her father. When I suggested an appropriate quote she just laughed out loud and said, 'He's not worth that! I'm just doing it to get some attention for my business.'

But of the all situations I have come across, one has stayed with me. It still plagues me, even though my colleague tells me it is really trivial and doesn't deserve all this angst.

Two years ago, a man in his mid-fifties came to the office; he had grey hair and was wearing a gold chain around his neck with a pendant made of blue gemstone. He asked us to publish an obituary, and having registered the gold chain, I automatically presented him with some of the ready-made Christian templates. They all seemed no different to the empty utterances I used to hear in the village: 'He lays at the mercy of God's judgement,' 'With Christ he is at peace,' etc. He smiled at me weakly and said, 'I want a eulogy for a dead Muslim.' I flinched, apologised and pulled out the Muslim templates. He chose 'O peaceful soul, go back to your maker' – a popular choice for the bereaved placing an obituary in a newspaper. Everyone wishes for their loved one's soul to rest in peace. I should say, more precisely, that some wish for it, while others don't really care. I told him to sit down and make himself at home then presented him with the various options. He chose what he wanted quickly – the most expensive option – and he paid straight away as his eyes welled up with tears.

I asked him for the details of the obituary: the deceased's name, the next of kin and the longer text he wanted in the obituary. He gave me all the information promptly, almost as if he had known it by heart! However, something caught my attention, the name of the deceased. I asked him 'Isn't she the famous dancer?' He nodded from beneath a silent stream of tears.

I replied with disdain, 'You want that vulgar belly dancer's soul to rest in peace?!', adding 'What strange times we live in!'

Before I knew it, I was on the floor, head bleeding, while my colleagues were trying to pacify the bereaved man, who left and took his money with him.

I sat back on my desk; my colleague looked at me accusingly and asked, 'How do you think you can judge what will happen to people after they've died?'

Everyone dispersed and I was left on my own, neglected. Even though I was angry at this man, I also felt some guilt tingling inside me. I felt that I had let my words come out from deep inside me, into the vast space outside. Now everyone had heard them, and they had led to some people despising me and others despising the dancer! Regardless of the two camps, the hatred that had been unleashed was my fault.

I never found out whether the man published the obituary elsewhere, or simply abandoned it. All I knew was that the pain kept growing inside me until it had become a permanent resident. I cried a lot, I asked God for forgiveness; I even went as far as asking for a transfer to another department.

I just wished that I could meet the man again, to ask for his forgiveness. Eventually, in my searches for him, I discovered that he had played music in the dancer's backing band, and that he'd died a week after her.

I came up with a solution to put my mind at ease; I took the obituary options he wanted and paid the charge myself. I put up an obituary for both of them, which was published. But my pain has still not subsided.

Notes

1. *Carat* – an area of land equivalent to 175 square metres.
2. *Bandar* – a term used by people in the countryside to refer to the city, or the market-place, or city centre.
3. *Fajr* prayer – meaning 'dawn prayer', an obligatory ('Subuh') prayer with two rakat (prescribed movements), and one of the five daily prayers offered by practicing Muslims.
4. *Dhuhr* prayer – 'noon' prayer, also known as the Zuhr prayer.
5. *Mish* – a traditional rural side dish made from cheese that has been fermented for months and sometimes years.
6. *Isha'* prayer – evening or night prayer.
7. *Eideya* – a monetary gift given to children on the occasion of Eid, could also mean a general celebration monetary gift.

Into the Emptiness

Hassan Abdel Mawgoud

Translated by Thoraya El-Rayyes

I DROPPED THREE CUBES of sugar in a glass of tea and they vanished before I could even stir them. It is said they disappear into the emptiness between the particles of tea. I thought about how I, too, dissolve in this world and disappear. Then, that sound snatched me out of my thoughts again. I ran to the door and looked through the peephole to see (finally!) my neighbour's huge frame kicking the bin bag, throwing it in front of him, then stomping on it. From where I stood, I could hear the clatter of cans, chicken bones and stale bread succumbing beneath his heavy feet. I opened the door quickly, but – in an instant – he disappeared as if he'd evaporated, or flown through the ventilation shaft at the top of the stairwell. The intestines of the black bag had spilled onto the floor. I ran past – careful not to trample the bag – and leapt up the stairs, but there was no trace of him. I looked up at the sky, half expecting to see him flying away.

How long had I lived in this neighbourhood? Maybe three years. The vast stretch of desert surrounding us had started to shrink. Buildings sprung up quickly, as if multiplying. The sounds of cement mixers, bulldozers and cranes had become my friends over the years, my companions in moments of loneliness. The contractors finished their work quickly, like beasts devouring the sand that used to extend far into the distance. Here, in Sheikh Zayed, everyone works to brush the sand away into the backdrop. Sand has become a distant memory to us and only springs to mind when we happen to see it from our cars, driving through the furthermost exits and entrances to the city.

Three years had passed without once meeting my neighbour face to face. I would only see him when he threw bin bags off the balcony. I was shocked at this impatient behaviour, the bin men were never late in collecting the rubbish. I formed an impression of him derived entirely from his size. Having never been able to make out his features, which – from a distance – always seemed blurry on that gigantic face, I concluded they must be very delicate, unlike the immensity of his face, of his body, his limbs. I used to imagine the balcony collapsing under his enormous weight. He didn't seem to do anything but throw rubbish onto the pavement and attack my bin bags. The bin men don't clean up mess. Their job is to collect the bags; the scattered rubbish isn't their problem. This morning was my first chance to put a stop to this, but he vanished into emptiness.

From my window, I caught a glimpse of him above, looking down at me through his own window. I startled, terrified. As he stared at me, a smirk appeared on his lips. Or so I imagined. Opening the window, my fear turned into anger, and I started to wave my arms and yell at him, telling him to stop attacking my bin bags. But he stayed still as a statue, then closed the curtain. How had he gotten down to my floor and climbed back up to his so quickly? He must have been hiding somewhere. Maybe he'd been watching me from that hiding place and when he saw me enter the building started quietly creeping towards my bins. I'd once seen a film where the actress and her son turn out to be ghosts at the end, the world they'd been terrified by was the real world. Could my neighbour just be a ghost, or am I the one playing the ghost? I laugh at the idea. Who knows how long I will keep on thinking of myself in this way. I am sure that I'm alive, there is plenty of evidence. It's true, there is no one to ask after me – I don't have any parents, friends, loved ones. I've chosen isolation. Even work colleagues who tried to befriend me came to realise I am a wall that cannot be penetrated by pleasantries. I intentionally hurt their hands when they try to shake mine. The features of my face are hard as stone. Sometimes I even practice scowling in the mirror. It didn't take long for them to distance themselves. Despite all this, it is they – more than anyone – who confirm that I truly am a living, breathing being. I see them every day at work, and their existence makes me feel certain that I'm here.

The cars that drive alongside me on the highway from Sheikh Zayed City to Cairo, where I work, also let me know that I am alive. I'd often imagine that I was a dead man driving a car that no one else could see. More than once, I'd switch lanes only so that other drivers would hurl curses at me. At that point I'd return to my lane, smiling and reassured. Whenever the thought of death took hold of me, I would turn on the television and turn up the volume, or pick up my phone and go online. Incidentally, the contact list on my phone only contains a few names: my manager who I sometimes have to inform I'm sick and can't come in, and a few tradesmen – a plumber, a carpenter, an electrician. I deal in job titles, not individuals. I save people's phone numbers according to their functions – administration, electricity, carpentry, plumbing and so on. Sometimes, I have an urge to dash to the balcony and point the car key out into empty space. When my car beeps, I feel comforted. Sometimes when I do this, my neighbour quickly appears and imitates me, the sounds of the two cars intertwining. I occasionally feel irritated by this, but in the end I usually decide that it comforts me. But then, from time to time, I come other across things that make me feel like I'm far from normal. Either I am, or that the whole world is far from normal. I feel like my neighbour – who I don't know anything about – only exists to make me feel like I don't exist. When he appears, I start to search for evidence of myself. Once, I asked one of the bin men about him. He said he didn't know anything about the man, then started to go on about how stingy he was. Excitedly, the bin man told me about the times he was sure the neighbour was home and would keep knocking on the door. He swore that the neighbour would make sure he could be heard moving about in there, but wouldn't answer because he didn't want to give him a tip. He said that just because the neighbour throws his rubbish off the balcony, it doesn't mean he doesn't have to pay because they still have to pick the bags off the street.

I've had many strange experiences in my life. When I first showed up for my university exams, I found the examination hall empty. The staff there told me the exam had been the day before and I almost exploded. I swore to them that I'd copied the timetable down correctly. From their facial expressions, they clearly thought I was insane, everything I said completely contradicted them. We walked over to the noticeboard and found that the timetable was just as they'd said. One of them angrily told me that they were not conspiring against me, and that it would have been absurd to rearrange the schedule and tell all the students except me in particular.

All my classmates at university worked under the assumption that I was strange. I used to say – when I saw this on their faces – that it wasn't a problem, that I believe everyone has a role to play in relation to others. We always prefer to reduce people to a single trait, one that we let overshadow their other characteristics. We say someone is good or evil, intelligent or stupid, sunny or sour-faced, normal or strange. I used to think it was others who were strange. A guy – to give an example – who insists on always laughing is very odd to me.

But apparently not. Still, I believed they were entitled to see me that way, as long as I also allowed myself to think of them *my* way. I would always pray that I'd get good marks at university because this would mean I'd be able to control my life, for instance, that I'd be able to control the number of people I would have to deal with. There are hundreds of students and professors at university, but after that you can reduce the number considerably, especially if you choose the right career. Without hesitation, I chose to work in a lab. So my colleagues set papers down in front of me, which I look over and give instructions about in as few words as possible, before forwarding the samples on to doctors. I had no desire to get married, nor was there anyone in the picture likely to force me into it. I look at sperm samples all day – thousands of beings desperate for a chance at life – and marvel at how concerned people are with replicating themselves – this hunt for miniature versions of yourself. I think about how amoebas do it the best way because they ensure their survival by splitting. I don't know if amoebas ever experience orgasm, and I don't care what scientists think – I like the idea of endless self-division. The world branches off into thousands of different lines. I used to think I was delirious. So I told myself that I definitely *was* delirious and stopped looking at all the samples surrounding me.

To pass the time, I would watch movies, TV shows and sports. Back then, I felt an urge to follow the national football team. There was a general fever in the air, with everyone waiting for a decisive match that would qualify the team for the World Cup if they won. The team did in fact win, but nothing happened. The expected scenes of joy weren't shown on TV; instead the stations just showed their regular shows. The next day, I was shocked to read a newspaper headline: 'National Team in Crushing Defeat'. I didn't understand. I read the article and stared at the photo, at the look of pain on the players' faces. Terror closed in on me again, what did this mean? I'd watched the game. The team had won, those tearful players in the photo had been jumping for joy before my very eyes. I stopped one of my colleagues and asked him, 'The team lost?' The colleague answered – with a look of disbelief that I was even asking – by nodding his head. I felt like I wanted to cry, or to stop him again and ask: 'Do you really see me? Do I exist?' I was walking down the street, traffic was moving slowly and, at that moment, something thudded to the ground next to my foot. It was a small red parcel, I picked it up and smelled it, looking around at the stationary cars. All of their windows were closed. Someone must have thrown this hashish out of a window. So be it. I put it in my pocket and walked on. At home, I smoked two joints in a row and thoughts started to jostle in my head. The idea that I was descending from a mountain took hold of me, I couldn't stop. Of course, the steps I was trying to control broke into a run, then I was flying, then there was a painful collision between my body and some rocks. I got in the shower and drank two cups of coffee back-to-back but my mind wouldn't stop racing. I prayed to God to get me out of this mess in one piece, promised him I wouldn't smoke hashish again; all I wanted was to go back to my normal self. I don't know how people feel when their minds run with such terrible energy. When the doorbell rang and I answered it, it was the bin man. As soon as I saw him, I yelled 'I'm dead! I'm dead!' The man mumbled a few words as he looked at my lower half, then quickly left. It was then that I noticed I was completely naked.

Just as I got home from work one day, I decided to change something about my life. Seeing my neighbour, touching him (shaking his hand to be precise), seeing the wrinkles (if there were any) on his face, or the scars, the creases in his trousers, the scent of his sweat or cologne – it would mean that things really were normal. I knocked on his door, but he didn't open.

I waited on the balcony until I saw him coming up. Our eyes met, and he decided to stop and stare at me. Surely, he would need two or three minutes to climb up to his flat on the fourth floor, passing by me on the third. I quickly left the balcony, opening the flat door. Minutes passed slowly but he didn't appear. I thought about returning to the balcony until an idea popped into my head: that the neighbour was hiding downstairs. I walked down the stairs and surveyed the stairwell, but there was no trace of him. I looked through the ventilation shaft to where he'd been standing and saw a cat playing with something that I couldn't make out. Unintentionally, I raised my eyes towards his flat and saw him looking at me. I reckoned that a thin smile had taken hold on his face. Again – seemingly not for the last time – I felt panicked. Now, I was sure the neighbour was a ghost. Then I thought about the victory of the national team, and how everyone had acted as if they'd lost and just like that – again – the obsession invaded me: the problem wasn't with the world; clearly I was dead but was refusing to admit it to myself. It was true I could touch things and taste them, hear people's voices, and that others responded to my voice, but there was something off about it all. I couldn't stop the thoughts, like handkerchiefs – each tied to the end of the last – pulled out of a magician's pouch, endless and terrifying. I looked out the window. At that moment, the weather was glorious. Despite everything, it seems, we still can't quite eradicate the desert. Signs of it appear whenever the winds starts up. It gathers in the cracks of the tiles surrounding our garden, making the plants looking like an army of invaders trying to defeat it. Even these thoughts mean that I am still thinking. Dreams are more like death, devoid of background. If I were dwelling in the other world, I wouldn't be seeing images so vividly. In this desert city, images are thick and colour is everywhere. Age gives Cairo its ghostliness, that grey that has seeped into Cairenes' faces is what makes the city more dream-like, more death-like. It's all the same. I contemplate the signs for doctors' clinics here, in this suburban city, and in Cairo. In this desert city, the names are incredibly clear – as if the signs had just been written, making you feel as though it were a city of doctors who have just come off a factory assembly line. In Cairo, the names disappear behind that miserable grey. On the 6th of October Bridge, they fade behind the cancerous buildings. Everything out here should make me grateful since it is evidence of my life, but I can only find myself in Cairo. People in Cairo are consumed by anger, maybe it's the sheer number of them that comforts me. It's enough to step on someone's foot for him to trample you with curses. So I decided to become more focused over the coming period, and watch one of the soap operas that the media said a lot of people were watching. At least one of my colleagues in Cairo must be watching it. A grim, boring episode, as it turned out. The dark-skinned character – one of the main ones, as I understood it – died in an accident. The next day, I brought it up with my colleagues when the lab was quiet. They looked at me with amazement, especially when I told them about the character's death. Two out of the three had seen it, and assured me that the character hadn't died. 'Why would they kill off one of the main characters?' one of them asked, snidely. 'You're obviously delusional!' added the one I'd asked about the football earlier. Before I left the office, he brought me a newspaper and pointed to a summary of that night's episode, which showed a photo of the dark-skinned actor. He assured me that the character would marry the girl he loved, despite her family's opposition.

I considered suggesting that I watch a match or an episode of the soap opera with them. Maybe an episode of a talk show, or even a cooking show. But I didn't. As I drove home that night on the highway, I imagined I would no doubt see one of the players score a goal, while they simultaneously saw him miss the target. I would pretend to be happy, even though I don't like football, while they would bury their faces in their hands, not because they support the other team but because they would be watching something different. Cars were driving past me at different speeds. Some shot off like the wind then disappeared, as if we were in a race. The image of the three sugar cubes disappearing into the tea flashed in my mind, then I saw a car drive up next to me. It was a police car, then I noticed a policeman on a motorcycle on the other side. I had to slow down and pull over on the side of the road. At that moment, I knew that the radar had picked up how incredibly fast I had been driving. I felt intensely happy. I patted the shoulder of one of the officers and apologised profusely. Apparently, this was too much because the officer glared at my hand, so I lifted it quickly as I mumbled 'Sorry!'

The Other Balcony

Nahla Karam

Translated by Andrew Leber

As SOON AS HE TOLD me they'd be moving into the building facing ours, I began dreaming of what it would be like to be able to see him whenever I wanted. This was after the school found out about our relationship, when they moved me from the class where we had studied together to another, all-female group. I had barely seen him since.

Now that he was our neighbour, I thought, his mother and mine would surely become friends. The more they visited each other, the easier our relationship would be – once we were old enough and he had asked for my hand in marriage, our families wouldn't need to get to know each other; we would all merge into one big clan.

On the day itself, I returned from school to find a removal van loaded with furniture in front of the building across from ours. Smiling, I ran up the steps of our house and went out onto the balcony of my room, not even pausing to change out of my school uniform. I gazed up and found him standing on a balcony that looked out on ours, smiling back at me.

He waved and said something I couldn't make out, even after he had repeated himself many times. Seeing me shake my head once again, he left for a bit, then returned with a piece of paper. He flattened out the paper on the wall behind him, scrawled something across it, then folded it into a clothes peg and tossed it down to me.

I chose this room so you'd be the first thing I see every morning.

I looked at him with a smile and he said something else I couldn't make out, so he wrote it down again and threw it over with another clothes peg.

I need to go help the workers – see you soon.

My smile disappeared when I heard the sound of my father and mother arguing, and my heart raced, hoping they wouldn't get any louder. The two buildings were very close together, after all. I had to go in and close the window behind me to keep the noise down a little. What if he heard the sound of their constant fighting? (I hadn't taken this into account when he told me he was going to be our neighbour.)

As soon I woke up the next morning, I jumped out of bed and headed out onto the balcony. I saw him standing there. He tapped the watch on his wrist, which I took to mean he was saying I had woken up late – and that he needed to go. Before he went, though, he made a circular motion around his face and gestured towards me, smiling.

I didn't understand what he meant, and he hadn't written anything to throw down to me. When I went into my room, however, I looked at the mirror and was shocked to see myself. *Did he mean my frizzy hair?*

When I woke up the next day, I didn't leap straight from bed to balcony, but went to the mirror and straightened my hair first. He was waiting when I finally went out, but he wasn't smiling. He gestured at me again, waved his hand as if to ask a question I didn't understand, then wrote yet another note thrown down with a clothes peg:

How can you go out on the balcony dressed like that?

I always wore my sleeveless pyjamas and shorts in the summer, but, at that moment I felt like I had stepped outside naked. I slowly looked up at him, not making any signs with my hands, then lowered my head back down towards the street. After a while, I heard another clothes peg bundle land at my feet.

Don't get angry at me – I love you, and I don't want anybody but me to see you wearing that outfit. Wear it if you want to but just don't go out onto the balcony.

I nodded my head in agreement, thinking maybe I should buy some new pyjamas for the next time I went on the balcony.

I didn't just change the clothes I wore; I also started to do my hair whenever I went out onto the balcony – sometimes pulled back into a bun, sometimes in rolls. I'd straighten it even if it was still wet, so Kareem wouldn't see it looking messy. Even when I wasn't feeling well – he might come out onto his balcony at any time.

I always tried to look my best in front of him, even when we spring-cleaned our apartment – the first time we had done so since he and his family moved in. My sister and I had a system, dividing up the rooms for cleaning; I would always pick my own room and the living room because they had the least furniture to clean around.

I scrubbed and dusted the entire room, but before I crossed the threshold onto the balcony I realised I was wearing a dirty dress and had a handkerchief wrapped around my head to keep the dust out. I had always gone out onto the balcony dressed like this on cleaning day, but suddenly I felt that I couldn't do it anymore, now that Kareem was above me. I went over to my sister – in the middle of cleaning the other room – and asked her to wash down the balcony after she had finished up her section, claiming that I felt too exhausted. But she refused – I had chosen the room with the balcony, so I had to clean it as well.

I went back to my room in despair, hiding behind the curtain and sneaking a look up. No Kareem. He might not be home at all; I hadn't seen him since the morning. So I decided to clean the balcony quickly before he came back.

When I had finished, I crouched down to sweep the dirt into the dustpan. At that moment, I heard Kareem's mother from inside their apartment. Confused, I looked up just in time to see his back as he headed inside. I dropped what I was holding and ran to the mirror, squatting down in front of it to try and imagine what I looked like from above. What had I been doing when he showed up?

After washing and straightening my hair, I stepped out onto the balcony every so often to try and erase the memories of what he'd seen before. But he didn't come out again until nightfall; he just made one gesture and didn't say anything. We normally didn't speak at night. I had been learning his sign language since he moved in, but the dark made it difficult to understand. Still, I was quite cross when he went back in as soon as he finished his cigarette – not a word or a clothes peg.

I stayed up all night wondering: had he been able to see me through the darkness in my clean clothes, with my straightened hair? Or did he think I was still dressed like I was in the morning?

From then on, I started going to the balcony in my outdoor clothes, standing outside for long periods of time so that Kareem would see me if he came out. Perhaps he would remember what our relationship had been like before he moved to the neighbourhood. But he no longer came out to the balcony quite as often as he had in those early days.

I caught sight of him by chance once, outside of the hours I was used to seeing him. I tried to make what I thought was a questioning gesture, not really expecting a response. Still, he wrote me a note:

I don't spend much time at home these days – I go out to study with my friends because exams are coming up.

I nodded my head even though I wasn't convinced – I knew he was the last person to be interested in studying.

I decided then to focus on my own studies and stopped going out onto the balcony much. I pulled the curtain back far enough that I could still see him if he came out, but so that he couldn't see me. Still, he didn't appear all that often, and when he did would head back in as soon as he had finished his cigarette without so much as a glance in my direction. I knew that something had changed but convinced myself that it was because he was focusing on the exams. I figured I would wait to speak to him when they were finished.

The day after exams, my mother decided that we were going to clean the apartment from top to bottom – during our exams my sister and I hadn't been doing much cleaning. This time, I chose another room that wasn't mine, but came running back in when I heard my mother shouting.

I was surprised to find her arguing with Kareem's mother when I came in. My mother had started to beat out the carpets on the balcony and Kareem's mother had come out to complain about the dust rising up towards her laundry; the two buildings were very close together. My mother then took this opportunity to remind Kareem's mother that she, too, cleaned her balcony without letting us know – not giving my mother any time to keep the dirt off her washing, even though this was the first time she had complained about it.

The argument grew louder as they continued trading accusations. Before that point I had assumed they didn't know each other – I had longed to see the moment when they met and became friends. Unfortunately, I learned that they had come to know each other in a totally different way. Each had been nursing an anger and resentment towards the other.

Eventually, our neighbours were able to calm them down, and the whole affair ended without Kareem appearing on the balcony. I had hoped he was out at the time, and hadn't heard any of their argument, but when she went back inside, his mother angrily called for him. He must have heard.

The next day, I went onto the balcony as soon as I saw Kareem from behind the curtain. I waved, and he returned the greeting without a smile. I brought out a book and pointed to it as if to ask how the exams had gone. He nodded his head, which I took to mean he had done well, and I waited for our conversation to start. But he didn't throw a clothes peg down – only gestured that he was going to head back in. I stopped him with a wave of my hand and wrote something out in large letters, certain he hadn't understood the question:

What's with you?

He shook his head as if to say it was nothing, so I wrote out again:

Write to me

And so he threw me a clothes peg:

I'm telling you… there's nothing with me

I held up the *What's with you?* sign again, and kept holding it up as I waited for some other answer. He threw down another piece of paper:

You've changed a lot… I don't know how to explain it, but that's how I feel.

I grew annoyed, wrote to him – *How?* – and waited for a reply. Yet he threw down one last clothes peg that said:

I can't write after today because my mother is getting suspicious – she has noticed that her clothes pegs are disappearing. I'm going in now – we can speak when we meet.

After he left, I became even more annoyed, and wanted to write him a sign that said *he* was the one who had really changed – and didn't love me anymore. We didn't need to let the arguments between our mothers affect our relationship! I hadn't changed at all, and still loved him as much as the first time we got to know each other! But I couldn't say anything. It would have been easy for him to toss down a page containing all those words from up there, but difficult from where I was.

Afterwards, we didn't agree on a time to meet like he'd said we would, and I no longer saw him on that balcony. Instead, I'd see his father stroll out for a smoke every evening – clearly they had changed rooms, and the room facing me now belonged to his parents.

Some time later we met by chance at a cleaning supply store. He said hello and told the cashier to take my order first, even though he had arrived at the till before me. I insisted they take care of Kareem first, but the cashier went off to do something, leaving us alone. We said nothing to each other in those few awkward minutes.

Kareem paid for his things. When he took the change, he pulled out a loose banknote from his pocket and asked for some clothes pegs. He grabbed them with his free hand and said goodbye. For some time after he left, I wondered why he needed the clothes pegs if he'd stopped throwing messages down to me – and started to wonder what the other balcony in his apartment might look down on.

Two Sisters

Eman Abdelrahim

Translated by Ruth Ahmedzai Kemp

When I close my eyes, I see you in the gloom.
You're always with me, in every single dream.

I

IT WAS LATE, AND all was quiet in Maadi. Every street looked the same: almost deserted. Not unusual for that time of night. I was wearing a tracksuit and Activ flipflops, and carrying two video cassettes on my way towards the rental shop around the corner.

I entered the shop and I saw that the enormous guy who worked there – a giant of a man with a hunched back, massive, ugly features and a long plait that dangled down his neck – was alone behind the counter. He looked like the Hunchback of Notre Dame in the shop's dim red lighting.

I said hello and handed him the video cassettes. He smiled and asked what I'd thought. I'd enjoyed them both, I said. I hesitated, then asked after his colleague, the one with the iron mask. A look of distress appeared on his face, and he told me, with a hint of sadness, that his colleague was suffering from depression these days and preferred to be alone.

He seemed kind, this giant with his hunched back. I liked the silver ring on his finger – and its huge green stone. He smiled at me the whole time we talked.

Unlike him, his colleague was a man of very few words and a constant frown. He had a slim, sporty build and beautiful, bronzed skin. An iron mask covered half of his face and the other half was scarred and distorted. You could just about make out his yellow eyes and his sharp lips amidst his doughy flesh. I stared at the left side of the counter where he usually stood. It was strange not to see him there. His absence left a great void in the shop.

The giant guy – the one with the hunched back – noticed I was distracted, and asked if I had time to stay for a chat; there were some things he wanted to talk about. I agreed straight away with an encouraging smile, and sat down on the chair in front of the counter.

He started to talk, becoming increasingly distressed – verging on tears – as he told me about his colleague's depression. He told me the guy was wealthy, and that he had once been very good-looking and completely fearless. He loved the movies and horse-riding, and used to work as a stunt double in Egyptian action movies. He had appeared as a double in most of the films in the video shop, he said. That was until one day when there was an accident on set: his face was splashed with a chemical which caused horrible scarring. As well as other side effects. Intrigued, I asked about these other side effects. He hesitated a moment, then told me that the only thing his colleague could eat was meat... raw meat... and that if he couldn't find any in time, he had to resort to eating human flesh. He then he corrected himself quickly, insisting that this had never actually happened, but that he was always desperate to get hold of meat, in huge quantities.

I laughed, assuming he was joking. The hunchbacked man didn't say anything. I asked him if this was the plot of a film that had just come out and if so could I borrow it? But he stayed silent. I didn't say anything for a few moments either, then I smiled and told him that I actually already knew. He looked at me in surprise. Or rather, I added, I knew that all of the films in the shop were all somehow part of him, or that he was part of them. He smiled and apologised for taking up my time, handing me a new video to borrow.

On my way home, I made a decision.

I went back to the shop the following day, to return the video I'd borrowed. The man with the iron mask was there this time, standing behind the counter on his own. I walked up to him with a smile. He reached out to take the cassette, and I took his hand. I looked straight into his eyes and revealed that I had feelings for him. I knew all about what he was going through, I explained, and I wanted to be always at his side.

He pulled his hand away from mine gently and turned to look away from me. He spoke very softly, telling me that he appreciated my feelings, but a relationship between us was impossible at the moment. Because I was normal and he wasn't. He might be forced to devour me if he ran out of meat in his fridge. I laughed and told him that I would be delighted.

When I insisted, he finally agreed, on the condition that I became like him. Then he wouldn't be able to devour me.

He led me over to a door at the back of the shop. I had never noticed it before; covered with the same wallpaper, it blended into the wall. He opened the door and we went into a small room with a bathroom off it. It was simply furnished with just a brown sofa and a small coffee table, a TV screen and a cupboard. Various belongings were scattered across the floor. He told me this was where he lived, sleeping on the sofa and watching film after film, never getting bored. I sat down on the sofa while he went to the bathroom.

He came back with a small black bottle. He sat down on the floor at my feet and took off my left flipflop. He dropped two drips of the stuff onto my little toe. I watched the toe sizzle and fizz as the acid ate away the flesh, until it was gone.

He noticed the silent tears on my cheeks and apologised for the pain he had caused me. I shook my head to say no, I was only crying because I was sad to see that little toe go. He rubbed my shoulders, telling me I now possessed that quality enjoyed by people of his kind – that *something* that he hadn't wanted to tell me about before my transformation, so that he could be sure that if I did it, it would be entirely for his sake.

We started meeting in his room on a regular basis. We'd sit there together on the brown sofa and chat. We'd laugh, watch films, have sex, eat raw meat. After a while he suggested we should get married. Without stopping to think, I agreed straight away.

*

I was in the hotel in my white wedding dress. The hairdresser had finished doing my hair. The make-up artist was just putting the finishing touches to my eyes, when my brother came in to tell me that they were all waiting for me in Room 37. As soon as I was ready, I realised I was ravenous and went quickly to join the others. I found my two brothers, my sister and my husband-to-be in the hotel room waiting for me.

My brothers had chosen to undergo the transformation entirely of their own will, when I had confessed the truth about us and told them about that *something* that set us apart. But my sister still didn't know anything about it.

I went over to my fiancé, to tell him how ravenous I was. He was too, he said, and so were my brothers; they had searched the hotel and the surrounding area for some raw meat, but hadn't found any.

Without meaning to, my gaze turned to my sister. I flinched when I realised. Then I saw that everyone was staring at her. I shuddered. I told them I was going to go quickly and find us something to eat. I asked my fiancé to look after my sister; he assured me he would, and promised that if things got bad, he would transform her to protect her. I couldn't bear the idea of her being transformed, too; I promised I wouldn't be long.

I ran through the streets, holding up the long train of my dress. I ran without stopping. It was midday and the sun was hot. I was worried that my make-up would run in the heat. I found a supermarket on the main street. I pushed the door open and went in.

The lights were off, except for one faint light from somewhere, I couldn't see where. The place was empty – no staff anywhere. I ran through the aisles, amidst rows of stacked goods. The supermarket was vast. I was looking for someone who worked there or for the meat counter. Finally, I found it. I stopped in front of the glass counter to catch my breath, unsure what to do. Someone tapped me on the shoulder to let him past, and I jumped. It was a tall man, a giant, and he walked around to stand behind the glass counter and serve me. I couldn't make out the top half of his body in the dark. He asked what I'd like; I asked for ten kilograms of filleted flesh. He started to cut the meat off the bone and chop it up, in the dim light from the lower part of the counter. I noticed he had a ring on his finger with a large green stone. I told him I didn't have time to wait, no need to cut off the fat.

I ran back and was out of breath when I reached the hotel room, clutching the bags of meat. I placed them on the table. I asked about my sister, and she came in from the balcony, smiling. I asked her to take off her shoes and, seeing that all her toes were there, all intact, I let out a sigh of relief. I went over to the bags of meat. I ripped them open and started to eat, as did my fiancé and my brothers. My sister came over and reached out her hand. She picked up a chunk and put it in her mouth. She smiled as she chewed, and the blood dribbled from the sides of her mouth.

II

Najwan couldn't forgive them for what they had done to her sister. She and her sister left at sunset to run away and get out of Cairo. She turned off the highway and parked the car in the middle of the rugged desert terrain. They both got out and Najwan grabbed her sister's hand as they began to run together towards the hill ahead of them where there was a cave. Najwan stopped every now and then to gather up the train of her dress which was dragging on the ground. They both stopped at the entrance to the cave, and her sister checked the map. It looked right according to the map, she said; they should go in and check. So, they went inside and Najwan's sister said they needed to find a door in one of the walls. They split up and started carefully feeling along the walls of the cave looking for the door. Her sister found it. She called to Najwan, her voice echoing off the sides of the cave.

Her sister gently opened the door. It led to a narrow stairwell, leading down, only wide enough for one person at a time. Najwan tried to see where it ended by peering down over the banister. It seemed to descend in a never-ending spiral.

Her sister entered first and started to go down the steps. Najwan tried to follow, but her puffy dress got in the way. She pulled off the bulky underskirt and draped the train of the dress over her left arm before following her sister down.

At the bottom they found a hall that was empty except for a door in the middle of one of the walls and an old caravan a few steps away from the door. Najwan's sister looked at the map in her hand, then walked over to the door. She knocked four times. At that point Najwan noticed a small sign on the wall next to the door. It said, *Do not knock on the door until you have stood in front of it for seven minutes.* She quickly pointed out the sign, and her sister stamped her foot on the ground; damn it, she said, they had lost it forever – that *something* that set them apart.

Najwan suddenly had an idea: she and her sister should split up, and one would take the map and hide behind the caravan, so that if the other sister was seized, she would let them believe she was alone. Then once they had gone, the other sister would try again, standing on the threshold of the door and waiting seven minutes before knocking. She would then finish the route and carry on searching without her. Her sister agreed and Najwan quickly went to hide.

The door opened and out came three old women with short, white hair, wearing matching green dresses. They grabbed Najwan's sister by the arms and dragged her in. Najwan saw one of the women peek underneath the caravan; she realised she had forgotten to hitch up the train of her dress. The women came over to Najwan, scolded her for trying to trick them, and dragged her with them too.

★

Najwan sat on the ground at her sister's side, hugging her knees to her chest, her back resting against the wall. The chamber was huge and mostly empty except for a few pillars stretching from the ground to the ceiling. Others were sitting on the ground, others who had lost that *something* – more than you could count. Some were leaning against the wall, some against the pillars. Najwan fought off sleep and forced her eyes open from one moment to the next. Her sister asked her in a whisper what was going to happen to them, and she replied that she didn't know, and that the girl next to her had said that they might be used for experiments.

A few minutes later, a man came in who was very good-looking, with a sporty physique and bronzed skin, wearing a white lab coat over grey trousers and holding a notepad and a pen. He took a pair of purple-tinted glasses from his trouser pocket and put them on. He asked everyone if they were pleased with themselves. Everyone said that they were not, while Najwan gingerly put her hand up and said that she *was* sometimes pleased with herself though other times wasn't. The man didn't write anything on his notepad. With slow, deliberate steps, he walked over to Najwan. He bent over her and stared into her eyes over the top of his glasses, noticing the yellow colour of her eyes.

'So, are you the solitary grasshopper in Green Belt Park?' he asked.

Without hesitating, Najwan answered this riddle with a 'Yes'. Then she fell into a deep sleep.

Siniora

Ahmed Naji

Translated by Elisabeth Jaquette

I MUST HAVE BEEN as crazy for her cunt as I was for the internet. Or maybe I was caught between the two addictions, my head somewhere in the middle.

I say my head and not my heart because this isn't going to be a romantic, erotic, or pornographic story; I don't want to exaggerate. I'm obsessed with cunts, generally speaking, but hers was my main fascination. Through all the years we were together I often just stared at it, and more than once I thought about taking pictures. But I was afraid of how she might react, so I held onto that desire, kept it secret and hidden like all my others, until things between us came to their utterly disappointing end.

It was still on my mind, and the thought of it brought me back to the days and nights I'd spent enthralled by all its fluctuations and transformations. I knew how it slept, with lips pressed together, and carefully noted how they opened, like the sun rising over a mountain range at the beach in Nuweiba.

I saw how blood pumped into the lips of her cunt when she was aroused, how they expanded and changed in colour from blush to deep pink to red. I saw how it changed during foreplay from the effects of my fingers and tongue; its colour fluctuated like a solar storm rippling across the surface of the sun when we fucked – and afterwards too. Smelling her was one of my greatest pleasures. Her scent changed depending on her mood and her cunt's mood. Sometimes when I woke up before her I would run to the bathroom, brush my teeth, rush back to bed, and slip my head between her thighs so that her cunt would be the first thing I smelled. I tasted it in different situations, noticing the flavour change as she became more aroused, as we lay in the shade of the guava tree of happiness. If I were to close my eyes and taste seven different cunts, I would recognise hers instantly, with just the tip of my tongue. It was somehow connected to all of my senses.

I should say that it wasn't just her cunt which drove me crazy, it was all of her holes. I used to ask her to lie on her stomach, with the pretense of giving her a massage. Before long I'd let my hand drop down, spread her buttocks wide, and take a deep sniff, walking my tongue between them. I'd fantasise that this moment could last for hours, stretching out into days, as Grace Slick's voice played in the background, gliding and permeating everything like the calmness of hashish slowly consuming your brain: now you're melting, the white rabbit is waiting for you at the entrance to the hole. Suddenly you're pulled out of this fantasy when you remember the building security guard downstairs. How did all this start again?

In one nightmare I was standing stock-still on the bank of a river while a huge pack of dogs slowly came closer, growling like monsters. The real predicament wasn't the dogs but me. I was petrified; my body had suddenly lost the ability to move. I was seized by an odd stubbornness and my legs began to tremble. Meanwhile in my waking life, things between us were starting to sour. There was a bit of screaming, lots of tears, and more than once she broke my heart. I felt like our happiness was fading away. Maybe we'd drank each other's last drop.

We broke up for a while, and I got a job as a salesman at a phone shop. I bought a car with a loan from the bank, put my energy towards building a successful life, made a new group of friends, learned to dance, and got into a car accident. When I woke up in the hospital with my left arm broken and lacerations to my face, I decided I didn't want this anymore. That night, I dreamed I was diving in the Red Sea; my tank ran out of oxygen and there was nothing around me to breathe from except her cunt, so I began swimming towards it, trying to reach it and inhale. I woke up from the nightmare with a chill, even though it was summer. I rolled myself a joint. Then I picked up the phone, called her, and asked: 'Have you ever thought about making hash yourself?'

A few days later we were sitting at the little table in my apartment. She said she'd only come because she was curious, and smiled. Meanwhile I crumbled the dried marijuana leaves she'd brought and patiently started to sift them. I got an orange plastic bowl, stretched a sheet of cheesecloth over it, placed a tea strainer on top, and started to crush the weed into the strainer while she smoked a cigarette and sipped her coffee. All conversation in the room was suspended. Eventually she broke the silence, trying to get me to talk, but I was afraid of saying the wrong thing, afraid of ruining the moment or making time move faster than I wanted it to. I crushed the leaves into the strainer, and they fell onto the piece of cheesecloth that I'd stretched across the bowl. I set aside the bits caught in the strainer, took the pieces that had passed through, and started crumbling them.

'What next?' she asked, encouraging me to speak, but I felt like I didn't have enough air in my throat. My soul was restless in my chest.

I started explaining what I was doing step by step: the point now was to remove all impurities in the weed, until we got to the flower. I shook the cheesecloth, and the green powder that had passed through the strainer fell into the bowl. 'Usually people do a 2:1 ratio of weed to henna,' I told her, picking up the henna. 'But we're going to try and do 3:1.'

I sifted the henna the same way, then mixed it with the weed and sifted the whole mixture again.

'And then? What next?' She asked again.

'In Sinai they don't add henna, which is why they get the green or light yellow colour,' I told her. 'They don't use molasses either in Sinai. In Morocco and Lebanon they dry and press the leaves. Those strains have a high resin content, so they don't need sticky additives.'

I got up from the table, came back with a jar of molasses, and went on explaining. 'As well as cutting the hash with painkillers and other chemicals, most recipes in Egypt don't use molasses, people prefer frankincense. We need to use molasses to knead the henna into the hash and bind it together. Without molasses or frankincense, you'll never get your hash to set in a solid piece, which you need if you want to smoke it Dabbous style.'[1]

'And you don't have frankincense?'

'Frankincense has a really distinctive smell. It makes the piece of hash tough, you feel it as soon as you take a hit, and if you put it in a joint it shoots sparks like a rocket.'

I smiled and pointed to a tiny burn hole in the T-shirt I was wearing. 'We don't want any more rockets, Koukou. We don't need any more pain and suffering than we've already got.'

I mixed the ingredients into a soft paste in the plastic bowl, took a razor blade from the table, using it to bring the mixture together in the container, then scraped it onto a piece of cellophane and began to shape it. I wrapped the cellophane around it tightly, then cut a piece of shiny silver foil and wrapped that around the cellophane. I looked over at her. A ray of sunlight from the balcony window spread through the living room and illuminated her face, making her look so pure. I felt an overwhelming desire to kiss her.

She smiled.

'And after that?' she asked.

I handed her a piece of foil. 'Can you put this in the oven, on low heat?'

She took it and headed to the kitchen, while I sat there staring at the chair she had just vacated. I remembered a dream where I was stranded in a foreign airport, with heavy luggage, in a city I didn't know. I was waiting for a plane that was supposed to arrive the following day, and then she appeared, driving a red car from the eighties. I heard her voice from the kitchen.

'What do you use to light the oven?'

I went into the kitchen. She was bent over, trying to figure out the oven. I walked up to her and put my arms around her from behind.

We decided we should still be on a break, and not to change the situation, but what was the situation again? I was diving in the Red Sea and suddenly my oxygen line was cut.

The second time she asked if she could go through the whole process by herself. She started by reading about different production techniques for hash and ways of processing marijuana. In the beginning we took what we'd concocted and smoked it together.

Then one time she made me an offer I couldn't refuse. We were waiting for the hash paste to set in the oven when, as if casually mentioning a visit to her parents, she said, 'Yesterday I went and had laser hair removal. They removed everything here.' She gestured between her thighs. While we had been dating she'd preferred just to trim her hair, I'd never seen her cunt without a light fuzz around it.

As if she knew where my thoughts were going, she made a sudden, new suggestion. 'I'm thinking we should sell it. Isn't it our own product?' She proposed a secret business partnership, based on friendship, benefits, and a love of cooking, which –

for her – was a complex hormonal ritual. She concluded her proposition by emphasising what we'd previously agreed:

'But this wouldn't change anything between us.'

She often disappeared for weeks without returning my phone calls or telling me what she was doing. When we happened to meet in public she would go for a handshake, reaching a hand towards me and preventing me from giving her even a friendly kiss on the cheek in front of anyone who knew us. One time she'd been in the middle of selling one of them a 'finger of hash' from a batch we'd cooked up together, telling a story about the 'ghost dealer' she worked with and who had many different kinds of products. I kept quiet, even pretended to be surprised.

At first she peddled this little tale about the 'ghost', but soon admitted to a close circle of friends that she was the one cooking the hash with her own recipe. By that point she'd started using a metal stamp with the word 'Siniora' etched into it. She pressed it into the paste when it was still soft, and the legend of the Siniora began to take shape.

To the outside world, she was known as Siniora Hashish. But my apartment, cooking headquarters, had become a temple where she appeared like a goddess of the city streets. She did the only thing I asked, the only condition I imposed from the moment the door closed behind her: she took off her clothes from the waist down. Then she sat on the sofa or the floor (she never liked the little table), spread her legs, and started to prepare the mixture. I'd hang around, smoking or picking out the music, my eyes glued to her shaved, hairless cunt, which glowed like a little sun. Our relationship – or 'things as they stood' – was pretty tenuous, fragile, the result of past events and old losses. Sometimes I thought that 'things as they stood' weren't one hundred percent real. Maybe they were a figment of someone's imagination, the daughter of an illusion, fantasies born of loss and loneliness. But I couldn't lose that pleasure, ephemeral as it was, so I didn't get too close or try to touch her. I was satisfied with the rules I'd imposed on our secret partnership, and as for her, she was satisfied with her share – the larger portion – of what we sold.

I discovered that she was skipping out on her day job, that she was thinking about quitting and starting some venture by herself, but she didn't tell me what it would be. She started making better quality products, raising the prices, and producing different varieties. Meanwhile, I took advantage of the space on my balcony and office to grow some plants myself. She told me how to care for them; fresher leaves meant a higher quality product in the end. She also started using a blender to liquify the leaves for pressing, which in turn produced a few grams of hash oil she could sell at a higher price.

She was growing bigger, developing, and a new life was opening up before her, or rather, a new religion was shining out on humanity from the temple that I'd established in my apartment and dedicated to her hairless cunt. I was an old man, searching for any religious myth that I could believe in until the end of my days, something that would give me some peace of mind.

Then she vanished.

I didn't hear from her for three months. It was the longest she'd disappeared from the temple since we'd started our partnership. Then a curt, decisive message arrived: 'There's no reason for us to meet again, we're eating each other up inside.'

I tried to go back to the person I'd once been but I didn't know who that was anymore. The world around me had completely changed. I decided to rediscover the present: I started going out, rekindling old relationships, gaining new experiences, feeling new pains, and all the while I kept tending to the plants. I didn't make hash, not even once. In my close circles, I started to hear about a new kind of drug called

'Siniora.' It was everywhere, and though it looked and smelled like hash, the high was different.

It was a slow burn; it didn't sting or hurt your throat, even when you smoked it straight, lighting a stick of it inside a covered cup and letting the smoke accumulate before inhaling, in a style called Alexandrian Khabour or Dabbous. Siniora also stood out for its concentrated oils and the pungent smell that clung to your hands afterwards. It crept into your brain slowly; it had the usual effects of hash, but it also brought on a state of pure joy, and a strange rush of feelings, as if it were releasing everything you had suppressed, turning the past into laughter, and soothing pain in the present. It filled you with the feeling of joking among friends, with kisses, and with visible, joyful love.

I tried the new product once and its effects took me by surprise, so I bought a piece and took it home. I tried to remember her process down to the last detail, but she'd used different mixtures and additives every time she tried something new. We were still in our partnership phase, and she was testing things out to find the best recipes. She'd tried so many different types of henna and molasses, and various kinds of fertiliser. She drew up a timetable that said when the plants needed to go in the soil. I felt like an idiot when I realised that I actually knew very little about her recipe. Throughout every stage of production, I'd focused more on the music, her legs, and her hairless cunt, waiting for the moment when she went to put the paste in the oven, so I could watch her ass sway like planets in orbit as she hummed the 80s Arabic pop song 'There Goes the Señora, Walking like That' and disappeared down the hallway towards the kitchen. I was lost in her beauty. I kept waiting, hoping she'd forgive me, counting how often she'd laughed when we met up. Every time she made a new recipe, she had me try the first joint and asked what I thought. She always recorded her little observations in a little notebook with a photo from 'Kill Bill' on the cover.

The newspapers dedicated whole pages to the drug they called 'Siniora': how dangerous it was to the economy, public health, and users' brain cells. Soon it was harder and harder to get hold of. I figured she was in the middle of a war with other dealers and the influential networks that ruled the country's drug trade. But she was slowly expanding her distribution, and her reputation was growing. One man, after his third hit of the joint, said: 'Siniora has come to save the world.'

I worked so hard to forget her, but every time I tried to leave the ruined temple where I lived to go interact with other human beings, the conversation turned to Siniora: who was she? What was the secret behind the hash she produced? Sometimes I felt depressed and just sat around at home, taking care of the plants and watching American movies on TV. One day I had a dream where the past imprinted itself onto the present. We were living together. Before Siniora, before I'd gotten so stubborn, before my legs started shaking. In the dream I was sleeping. She arrived home, came up behind me, and hugged me; and I had the feeling that happiness had been right there, in front of my eyes, the whole time. But I knew it must have taken a long, painful journey to get there. Strangely, we also had a massive dog in the dream, even though neither of us liked dogs.

I woke up from the dream crying silently, feeling a wave of acid rise from my stomach to my throat, when my cell phone rang and her name appeared on the screen. Months had gone by without any word from her. I stopped crying and pulled myself together before picking up.

'Hello. How's it going Koukou?' I asked levelly.

Quickly and decisively, just like she'd always been, she asked if we could meet. She set the time and said that she would come to my place, but not to tell anyone; her life was different now. 'This changes nothing between us,' she added before ending the call.

At first, when she walked into the house, I couldn't tell if she'd changed; maybe she'd been gone so long it just seemed like she had. Maybe the fact that she'd asked to come over was why I was smiling senselessly. She took a seat at the table, and we started to talk about trivial things. She took out a piece of hash I'd left and started to crumble it. 'Did you make this?' she asked with a smile, and I nodded. 'It's not Siniora-brand hash..., Siniora.'

She put her feet on the table in front of me. She was wearing a thin anklet around her left ankle, a slender silver chain that wrapped around her marble leg. Here and there, her skin gleamed in the light. Little spheres shaped like the nine planets dangled from the chain. Each one was hollow, with a smaller planet inside, so that when she shook her foot they rang like heavenly bells.

I handed her a rollie. She told me stories about her new world. Most of the time she lived on the Red Sea, between Ain Sokhna, Gouna, Safaga, and even Marsa Alam. She hardly ever came to Cairo – just to take care of 'business' as she said in English. 'Business' meant a series of partnerships with a 'franchise' of dealers and hash traders. She supervised the concoctions herself and lived off the revenue, but lately things hadn't been going well. The market wasn't straightforward, competition was fierce, and in order to get protection from the police she needed to give them something in return. To satisfy the public, the police had to make a show whenever they arrested an individual or network of people who dealt in Siniora. She told me she was thinking about leaving the country for a while, until things calmed down, but if she left the market now she wouldn't be able to get back in.

'And you? How are you doing?' she asked.

'I miss you – I want you.'

A torrent of confessions poured out of me; I may as well have surrendered completely. For a reason I still don't understand, I began telling her about a scene I remembered from years earlier; we'd been swimming at the beach in Nuweiba, and began to people-watch and chase the colourful fish. I'd reached out to touch one and was pricked by its spines. She'd been wearing a pink bikini. Her hair was a bit longer back then, and the water had made it cling to her body.

I began describing the fish as she drew closer to me, joining me, and my breath quickened as I embraced her. My heartbeat felt like it was pounding through massive speakers, my breath was racing, and she was pressed up against me, taking off my clothes, repeating 'Hush, hush,' as if she were calming a small child.

We were naked then, and our tears mixed with kisses, molasses, and saliva. Our bones cracked under the pressure of our embrace, our souls in our throats. We made love sadly. I just wanted to stay inside her, not moving, as if that would achieve the impossible: to freeze time. We held each other for several minutes after our half-ecstasy. Then she started getting dressed and muttered something like a goodbye.

I spent two days laying where she'd left me after she walked out the door. I felt like all the energy inside of me, all the desire for life, was gone. Eventually I managed to get up. I took a cold shower, went out onto the balcony, and started picking leaves from the plants growing there and in the apartment. I took out the equipment, put on an Oum Kulthoum song, and started cooking all the hashish I had in the apartment. I put the paste in the oven and then picked up the phone and made a call to a police detective. I took out the stamp engraved with the word 'Siniora', began stamping pieces of hash, and lined them up on the table.

I sat there smoking, dreaming of long walls and filthy surroundings, somewhere with no room for hope or dreams.

Notes

1. Alexandrian Khabour or Dabbous is a method of smoking marijuana resin by lighting the resin, placing it inside a cup, covering the cup to capture the smoke as it accumulates, and then inhaling the smoke directly.

Hamada al-Ginn

Nael Eltoukhy

Translated by Raph Cormack

*Dedicated to the lions and lion cubs of the
Egyptian Interior Ministry, with gratitude.*

EVERYTHING THAT MAJOR HAITHAM Hamdy did required
lightning-fast agility. A policeman has to be a man of electric
reflexes – a man of concentrated, focused and precise action.
Major Haitham Hamdy checked that he had holstered his
gun in his belt behind his back and went down to the street,
as he always did when he needed inspiration for a particularly
sensitive or complicated case. Finding himself sitting with a
cup of tea and a shisha pipe, he began to think.

This mission he had been charged with was clear. The
General had told him plainly that the youth were in terrible
danger:

'Everything is ambiguous and obscure; the youth of today
are full of doubts. You are only young, my lad. You don't
remember what it was like in our day; everything was
understood and well defined. People are confused now. The
Truth has gone missing and your mission is to find it again.
You have two days, Haitham, only two. We can't allow this
situation to become any more serious than it already is. I beg

you, Haitham. The entire future of our country depends on this mission.'

It had been a very long time since any challenge had shaken the State Security investigators like this one, the challenge of finding The Whole Truth, in its full extent: existence, death, life, morality, truth, justice, beauty. For many years their investigations had focused on smaller matters, confronting hostile activities and the surveillance of banned parties. But probing the question 'Where is The Truth?' that concerned the future of the entire country, that was something else. And, why entrust the search for the answer to the State Security investigators, in particular, and to just one promising, young Major? The state had tasked him with answering this question of utmost importance, and therefore safeguarding the nation's youth. The gravity of the situation made State Security, and the Ministry of Interior behind it, rather nervous but it also gave them the motivation they needed to succeed in the greatest challenge of its kind.

So... at three in the afternoon on the 16th August 2010, Major Haitham Hamdy was sitting in a shisha café, in plain clothes. Crossing one leg over the other, he began to think:

'The Truth must be complete, from Adam and Eve until... until... let's say, the year 3150. Also, The Truth has to be unified – its beginning must be connected to its end. I mean that I have to link Adam and Eve, Year Zero, to the year 3150. The Truth has to be shocking, since it exposes things that we were not aware of before, and it also has to be convincing – its details should logically follow on from each other. I don't think it is necessary that it has to be *real*. In other words, there is no obligation for the truth to be true; all of those previous conditions are more than enough.'

He dictated all of this, as a special report, which he then saved on to his mobile phone.

At half past three on the same day, Major Haitham Hamdy got up from his seat at the café. He was fed up – tired of the whole affair – so he left. The truth was always boring, and searching for it even more boring. But, no, a police officer could not be bored! A policeman is a creature of constant desire, he scolded himself as he climbed the stairs of his building.

★

Major Haitham Hamdy went back to his house that summer day in Ramadan, ready to prepare his Iftar meal (policemen fast just like the rest of us). After Iftar, he sat down to read some old case files (they also enjoy intellectual pursuits like the rest of us). Then he paced up and down (they pace too) mulling over the details of his other current investigation: Umm Amira al-Qar'a, Mahmoud Abu Khayra and Hamada al-Ginn.

Umm Amira, who owned an apartment building, had asked for Hamada al-Ginn's help evicting a tenant called Abu Khayra from it. In the process, Hamada al-Ginn had cut the man across his face with a pocket-knife and a huge fight had ensued, which somehow ended up with Abu Khayra's member being cut off with said pocket-knife. That was Abu Khayra's story, at least.

Umm Amira herself had a totally different story. Abu Khayra had not being paying his rent, despite her constant requests. In an attempt to get her off his back, *he* had sent Hamada al-Ginn to sort *her* out and he had opened up a gash on her head with the neck of a beer bottle. She then tried to

come at Hamada and, in an attempt to defend himself, he had
thrown a bottle of acid in her face, permanently disfiguring it.

One of them, Umm Amira or Abu Khayra, he supposed,
had injured *themselves* so that they could accuse the other and
had used Hamada al-Ginn as their agent (Or could he have
been a double agent? Perhaps Hamada al-Ginn had done both
of these deeds. Anything was possible).

Keeping Umm Amira and Abu Khayra locked up in the
police station did not uncover any new information. They
both stuck to their stories, despite the continuous physical
interrogation that they were subjected to for three days,
ordered by Major Haitham Hamdy himself (some people give
this 'physical interrogation' the name 'torture').

We should take the time to explain something here: it is
true that this physical interrogation is not strictly legal and it
is also true that Major Haitham Hamdy does sometimes resort
to it. But we should also say, firstly, that this does not poison
the entire police apparatus, which is renowned for its courage
and humanity, nor, secondly, does it even poison Major
Haitham Hamdy himself, who may have personal flaws like
any human being and, like any human being, may sometimes
be overcome by these flaws. Major Haitham Hamdy was a
human to his core, we have already seen how he fasts, how he
enjoys intellectual pursuits and how his mind wanders like
everyone else's. So, it is no surprise that every day and night
after reading the morning and afternoon reports he repeats
this phrase: 'I am a corrupt officer but I do not represent my
colleagues, honourable policemen, in any way. I am one man.
I am the exception. I am extraordinary. I am outside the herd.'

This torture (which some people call physical interrogation)
occurred right in front of the Major in the police station.
Perhaps he felt pain as he watched the torture or perhaps it
was a smile of pleasure, it was hard to tell exactly from his
expression. (Every person has their own particular look of

pain just as a smile of pleasure is different from one person to the next. In both states the hero of our story, that exceptional individual, the man who stands aside from the herd, is totally human; human, as we said, to his core.) Our policeman was conscious that he was an exception, an individual, that he had broken the mould, and this gave him a certain degree of confidence when he was interrogating a suspect. However, that confidence fell apart in front of Umm Amira and Abu Khayra. The one hope he clung to was Hamada al-Ginn, our dear double agent.

*

Ever since he was a child, our Major had dreamed of finding out The Truth. Now, he was actively looking for it everywhere: in churches and in mosques, in factories and in fields, in cafés and in bars. He did not eat. He read everything and asked all kinds of people about The Truth. He was a religious man. He prayed, fasted, and gave the correct portion of his money for Zakat. Still, moments of doubt and questioning creep into the life of every man of faith. At times like these, questions infiltrated the heart of this astute policeman. It could happen at any time, even in the holy month of Ramadan. The General had exploited this old spark of doubt in his officer when he charged him with this mission, on which the future of the country and the youth of the nation depended. The Major did not stint on his task; he increased the normal frequency of his rounds to ask about The Truth. He went back again and asked about it everywhere: the churches, the mosques, the factories, the fields, the cafés, the bars. The life of a policeman is hard, he must do a thousand things in a single moment.

*

On the 17th August 2010 Haitham Hamdy arrived at his office and ordered Hamada al-Ginn to be brought to him. He came, haggard and carried in by the investigators. The Major lit his cigarette and then he gave one to his guest and told him to sit down. He calmly asked what had happened on the 11th August. Hamada replied that he had got into an argument with a police officer, who had decided to take away his driving licence – Hamada was a microbus driver – and that the policeman had threatened him and forced him to go back home early. 'I couldn't sleep the whole night, sir. I thought so much about it that I could hardly breathe, sir. In the name of the prophet, if you know this guy can you get him off my back?'

Major Haitham Hamdy had never lied to anyone before and so he couldn't stand it when other people lied to him. This was the gravest of sins as far as he was concerned, a red line, the most disgusting thing in the world. His face went as red as a tomato, he grabbed his cup of boiling tea and hurled it in Hamada's face. Then, he leapt over his desk right on top of Hamada and screamed at him:

'You have a sister called Aya and your mother is called Husna. Your sister was walking around with that guy Mahmoud, we took a picture of them together in Muqattam. Your mother has been married twice, neither time happily. How about we bring her here and show her a good time?'

Policemen, like everyone else, sometimes lose their temper.

'Look, Hamada, I'm not angry with you.' The Major returned to his desk and lit another cigarette. He continued:

'You have been a great help to us before, we are well aware. But the people in your area don't know that you've assisted us and I don't think they would be very happy if they did.'

Hamada did not reply. He looked at the Major with his two worn-out eyes and smiled an enigmatic smile that the

Major did not understand. He spoke:

'Manners sir, you can't get anything out of me by force. If you are polite, sir, I will do what you want.'

★

Major Haitham Hamdy went back home to think. He went over the history of Hamada al-Ginn, the microbus driver with two bright, intelligent eyes who worked with everyone: the government, drug-dealers, both big-time and small-time, gangsters and terrorists. And he got away with all of that, only to be taken in for being a petty thug. This young suspect was the cleverest person he had ever met, either professionally or personally. Hamada al-Ginn, the inspirational legend of Cairo's al-Khalifa neighbourhood.

Sometimes, in our lives, there are moments of chance that happen without logic or connection. Sometimes they just happen because we will them to. Chance flies through the air and some people grab it, whereas others don't. It's not thanks to them but thanks to the speed of the wind, their direction of movement or the force behind the flight. Chance, as the proverb says, is a beautiful girl, riding a bicycle, with her hair flowing behind her, whose beauty we chase.

'Could it be possible? Really, was the world that small? No, it doesn't make sense… It might… No, it's ridiculous, stupid' and so on, and so on, and so on… For the fourth night in a row Major Haitham Hamdy could not sleep.

★

Four whole days and Major Hamdy still could not sleep. Four days investigating the case of Hamada al-Ginn and four days investigating The Truth, the new mission that had come to add misery upon misery and give him insomnia. He read – it has to be said – every magazine he could. In his fevered search for The Truth he read many tens of pages in the few hours he had. He opened the Old Testament, the adverts pages in *al-Masry al-Youm*, Sheikh al-Shaarawi's commentary on the Quran, Sheikh Sayyed Sabiq's *Fiqh al-Sunnah*, the last two Friday editions of A*l-Ahram* and some of the other Friday papers, Aid al-Qarni's *Don't Grieve* and Paolo Coelho's *The Alchemist*. He also read *The Kamasutra*, primary school maths books, middle school maths books, high school maths books! Then he read the *Stories of the Prophets*, *The Book of Revelations*, Anis Mansour's *Men Who Came Down from the Sky*, Mustafa Mahmoud's *Dialogue with my Atheist Friend* as well as some of the sci-fi mysteries published in *The Future File*.

He read it all, even though he was aware that the time he had to complete this mission was coming to an end. All while he was supposed to be investigating the case of Umm Amira, Abu Khayra and Hamada, and without having slept for four days. This overwork might explain the hysteria that came over him on the morning of the 18th August, as he was questioning Hamada al-Ginn. But this was never his own explanation for what transpired.

He entered and told the officer to stop the beating. He approached Hamada and, waving his cigarette in his hand, he calmly stubbed it out on his arm. A smell of burning flesh came from Hamada's arm and then a punch came to send him flying to the other side of the room. A bolt of electricity fizzed through the atmosphere. Hamada al-Ginn lay on the ground and Haitham Hamdy walked over to him. He kicked him in the face with his steel capped boot then he leaned over his body, putting his shoulders beside Hamada's head, who was sprawled on the ground and whispered:

'Hamada, don't think I am torturing you so that you will talk about Umm Amira al-Qar'a and all that nonsense.'

Hamada did not reply. He spat out a little blood and wiped his lips on his sleeve.

'No, Hamada. I am torturing you because I need something much more important from you.'

'.........'

'The Truth, Hamada, I want you to tell me The Whole Truth.'

He straightened himself up and his worn-out eyes started to twinkle.

'Why are we here? Where are we going? Why are we alive? What are we doing in this world?'

A long silence.

An even longer silence.

Finally, Hamada began to talk, slowly:

'Manners, sir. Be polite and I am yours. I will tell you everything.'

'.........'

'If you want to know The Truth, you have come to the right man. I'll tell you everything: where we came from, where we're going, the truth of the world – The world is hard, sir, and people like us get trampled if we live without understanding it. It's the law of the jungle in our world now. I will tell it to you straight, from the day that our Lord created Adam until the end of time, until the year 3150, God willing. Just treat me with respect. That way is better for you and better for me.'

'And what if you're lying?'

'You can test me out; put every word I tell you to the test. People like me don't live in this world because of the good will of our parents. I live because I know The Truth and I apply it in my life.'

'If you lie, Hamada al-Ginn, I will personally violate you. Remember Emad al-Kabir, Hamada.'[1]

The Major gave a signal and the two other officers left the room. Major Hamdy stretched out his hand to help Hamada up. Then he sat him down at his desk, gave him a cigarette and sent for a cup of tea. And Hamada began to tell his story…

The Truth! It was exactly how Haitham had imagined it would be. It came in its entirety, included everything within it and was unified, everything followed on from everything else, it was convincing. It might not necessarily have been *real* but it was certainly shocking, as it was not previously known to him. Hamada al-Ginn told it and Haitham Hamdy repeated it after him, then wrote it down. He didn't redraft any of it; he merely rendered Hamada's extremely colloquial speech in slightly more formal language. He also got out the voice recorder on his mobile phone. The precise wording of Hamada al-Ginn's speech should be preserved for posterity. For three hours he spoke, without interruption. Sometimes, surprised looks from the Major would force him to clarify certain points more specifically and angry looks would make him choose a slightly more moderate turn of phrase (for The Truth is always shocking). Haitham Hamdy spent the whole session astounded, sweating, with his mouth hanging open.

Only when Hamada al-Ginn had finished his speech did the Major close his mouth, take a deep breath and wipe the beads of sweat from his glistening, balding scalp. He stood up and hugged Hamada al-Ginn. Two tears welled up and dropped from his cheeks on to al-Ginn's shirt. Al-Ginn noticed and also started to cry.

They were both sobbing, wailing and weeping.

★

On the 18th August 2010, Haitham Hamdy was promoted to the rank of Lieutenant-Colonel. Lieutenant-Colonel Haitham

Hamdy learned an important lesson that day: that you can only get to the truth with good manners; you can't get it with force nor can you get it all by yourself. Once and for all he stopped using torture and moved from the camp of corrupt officers to the camp of honourable ones. On that day the State Security investigators concluded one of their most dangerous operations, achieving a decisive victory. They had managed to discover The Whole Truth about our lives, as Egyptians, as Arabs and as wretched human beings, standing in the snare of this wide existence.

Since that day, all Egyptian people have been marked by their deep knowledge. Since that day the Egyptian people have been the only people to know The Truth and they boast of it to all other nations. Since that day the Egyptian people have shown their gratitude and love to the State Security Services, their dear State Security Services. It is a love that will never end.

Notes

1. The sexual assault of Emad 'al-Kabir' by a group of police officers was filmed in 2006 and caused uproar in Egypt. Two policemen were convicted in 2007 and given three-year prison sentences.

An Alternative Guide to Getting Lost

Areej Gamal

Translated by Yasmine Seale

THE SPACE BETWEEN THE padlock's body and its loop. The lock
that no one bothers, no one breaks.

She doesn't sleep at night, not any more. For seven weeks
she has been cut off from the ordinary cycle of time. Sleep
comes only with the light and the birds, and the night is spent
awake. Cut off from the street, too: she is not a man. Many
things in life frighten her because she is a woman. Her friends
are asleep; everyone is at this hour. That isn't the point. It's
nearly time for the flight, the Lufthansa, but she has yet to
obtain that neat little stamp they press into passports to ease
the crossing from one sky to another. She had paid her visit to
the squat, decrepit building in the corner of the square[1], had
stood in the queues, put up with the cats strangely present
indoors, suffered the smells (the whiff of human waste on the
walls), tried listening to Beethoven (the piano sonatas), tried
reading snatches from the holy book she held in her pocket,
all the while moving from floor to floor, hunting for a kind
heart among the staff who might grant her the stamp. But she
failed at all that: the place did not lend itself to poetry; it had
no time for poets. She went home, her passport blank, and saw
herself moving ever further from the Lufthansa flight, from

the other passengers and other skies. Then the circle around her slowly started to turn.

She couldn't face a second attempt, not during the day. Instead she started making nightly trips to the old building, very late, as though driven to it. On the first night the place was asleep, though the cats had left prints in the dust on the landings and on the edges of steps. She walked up to where the clerks were usually stationed behind their desks, and thought that perhaps she was being driven to resolve the matter herself and steal the stamp. But as she drew closer to their floor she sensed them all there, as if they never left, but instead shifted papers between themselves without rest. Taking care of uncompleted tasks, perhaps. She climbed the last step and stood level with the room: the queues were there too. Everything was as it had been, except the noise, of which there was none: the scene was silent. She joined a queue. Soon she had reached the front of it, but the clerk did not look up, simply took the passport from her and passed it from hand to hand, then slipped it to another worker, who in turn moved it between his palms. In this way she found herself spinning in a half-circle between them, all performing the same gesture, but none stamping the passport, none giving it back.

At the point where the half-circle stopped, she retrieved her passport and was pushed to the exit. Not that anyone made her go, but the cats had gathered on the stairs and were producing a sound that made her shudder. Now she was out, and something told her that if she kept returning at the same hour, the stamp might then be hers, and the same something told her that those people were not workers but their souls, suspended in the air at night. You could tell by the awkward way, come morning, they sat at their desks. Joylessly. They dreaded the day, longing to spend it asleep. Even when it was over, their work done, they didn't make love to their wives or play with their children. They threw their whole lives to the cats in the morning, to sleep at night. Then the something added that knowing this would help her: only knowing this could she coax them into giving up the stamp.

It did not occur to her that the half-circle in which she spun would never end, that these nights only proved the futility of a scheme trapped in shadow. The secret visits went on, always on time, but not once were the salaried souls moved to give her the stamp. Her body became the perfect antidote to daylight, clinging to the act of swimming on a floor without water until the cats gathered and drove it out in the same way every night. She too was suspended, helpless to secure a place in the body of the Lufthansa plane, the distant traveller to other skies.

Notes

1. A reference to the Mogamma (roughly translated as 'the complex'), a famous government building on Tahrir Square.

About the Authors

Eman Abdelrahim (b. 1983) began writing on literary blogs. In 2012 she wrote the script for the Egyptian animated series *People from the Dragon's Eye*. This story comes from her first collection, published in 2013. In 2015 she won a Sawiris Cultural Prize for the book.

Hassan Abdel Mawgoud (b. 1976) is a writer of both fiction and non-fiction. He has published two novels and two short story collections. His novel *Cat's Eye* won a Sawiris Cultural Prize in 2005 and has been translated into German. His work of non-fiction, *Stories of the Monks of Wadi Natrun*, won an Egyptian cultural journalism prize in 2003.

Nael Eltoukhy (b. 1978) is a writer, journalist and translator. He has published one collection of short stories and four novels. His novel, *Women of Karentina*, was translated into English and published by the American University in Cairo Press in 2014. His Arabic translation of the Hebrew book *Rachel and Ezezkiel* by Almog Behar was published in 2016. He also works as a journalist at the independent news site *Mada Masr*.

Areej Gamal is a young writer and film critic. She published her first collection of short stories, *One Table for Love*, in 2014. The story feature comes from her second collection, *Churches Don't Fall in War*, published in 2017.

Hatem Hafez (b. 1974) is a writer, academic, translator and journalist. He has written eight plays and one novel, *Because Things Happen* (2009). The story featured here is from his first collection of short stories, *Biscuit and Molasses*. His second collection of short stories was published in 2017. Hafez has won several dramatic prizes, including the Best Play at the Festival of Arabic Theatre in 1996 for the play *The Final Act* and the Fawzi Fahmy Prize for Drama from Cairo University in 2009.

Hend Ja'far (b. 1985) is a writer and academic from Ismailiyya. She currently works in the Manuscripts department at the Bibliotheca Alexandrina. This story is from her first collection published in 2015 by Merit, which shared the second place in the Sawiris Prize (Short Stories by Young Writers section).

Nahla Karam's (b. 1989) first short story collection, *To Hang in the Air,* was published in 2013. Her story, 'Tale from the Back Lines' was one of the winning stories in a Goethe Centre workshop and she won a trip to the Frankfurt Book Fair. Her novel, *On Freud's Couch* was shortlisted for the Sawiris Prize in 2015. The story featured here comes from her latest collection, published in 2017.

Mohamed Kheir (b.1978) is a poet and prose writer. He has published two collections of poems in Colloquial Egyptian Arabic and one in Classical Arabic. He also published his first short story collection in 2008 and his first novel in 2013. The featured story comes from his second collection of short stories, *Blink of an Eye,* first published in 2014.

Ahmed Naji (b. 1985) is a writer and journalist who was given PEN/Barbey Freedom to Write Award in 2016. His first novel, *Rogers*, was published in 2007 and his second novel, *Use of Life*, was published in 2014. Nagi was arrested after an excerpt from his novel was published in *Akhbar al-Adab*. He was sentenced to two years in jail for violating public morality. The novel, *Use of Life*, has been translated into Italian and English. The story in this collection comes from his first collection of short stories, published in 2016 by Merit.

Mohamed Salah al-Azab (b. 1981) was chosen as part of the prestigious Beirut 39 group of young Arab writers in 2009. He has written four novels and two short story collections. He has also written scripts for two Egyptian films. In 2002 he won the Kuwaiti Suad al-Sabah Prize for the novel in 2002 and Egyptian state cultural prizes in 1999 and 2004. The featured story comes from his latest collection, published in 2016.

About the Translators

Kareem James Abu–Zeid has translated novels and books of poetry by Adonis, Najwan Darwish, Tarek Eltayeb, Rabee Jaber, and Dunya Mikhail for NYRB, New Directions, and AUC. His translations have won Pen Center USA's Translation Prize (2017) and Poetry magazine's translation award (2014), among other honours. His work as a translator, writer, editor, and scholar has earned him residencies from the Lannan Foundation (USA) and the Banff Centre for the Arts (Canada), fellowships from the Fulbright Foundation (Germany) and CASA (Egypt), as well as a National Endowment for the Arts Grant (USA). He holds a PhD in Comparative Literature from UC Berkeley, and also translates from French and German.

Ruth Ahmedzai Kemp is a British literary translator working from German, Russian and Arabic into English. She has translated novels by Fadi Zaghmout, Hanna Winter, Kathrin Rohmann and Yulia Yakovleva. Ruth graduated from the University of Oxford in 2003 and completed an MA in Translation and Interpreting at the University of Bath. She translates contemporary fiction, non-fiction (particularly history, travel and nature) and children's books.

Raphael Cohen is a professional translator and lexicographer. His most recent publication is the novel *Guard of the Dead* by George Yaraq (April 2019). He contributed to *Blade of Grass, An Anthology of New Palestinian Poetry* (ed. Naomi Foyle, 2017) and has translated a number of novels including Mona Prince's *So You May See* (AUC Press) and Ahlem Mosteghanemi's *Bridges of Constantine* (Bloomsbury). He is a contributing editor of *Banipal*.

ABOUT THE TRANSLATORS

Raph Cormack is a translator, editor and author with a PhD in modern Arabic literature. He is the co-editor *The Book of Khartoum*, published in 2016 by Comma Press. As well as other translations, he is currently working on a non-fiction book about the female entertainers of early 20th century Cairo, called *Martyrs of Passion* (to be published in 2020).

Thoraya El-Rayyes is a literary translator and political sociologist living in London, England. Her English language translations of contemporary Arabic literature have won multiple awards, and have appeared in publications including *The Kenyon Review*, *Black Warrior Review* and *World Literature Today*.

Basma Ghalayini is an Arabic translator who has previously translated short fiction for the Commonwealth KfW's Beirut Short Stories writers' workshop, and Comma's *Banthology* project. She was born in Khan Younis, and grew up in the UK until the age of five, before returning to the Gaza Strip.

Elisabeth Jaquette's translations from the Arabic include *The Queue* by Basma Abdel Aziz (Melville House, 2016) and *Thirteen Months of Sunrise* by Rania Mamoun (Comma Press, 2019). Her work has been shortlisted for the TA First Translation Prize, longlisted for the Best Translated Book Award, and supported by English PEN, the Jan Michalski Foundation, and the PEN/Heim Translation Fund. Elisabeth is also an instructor of translation and the Executive Director of the American Literary Translators Association.

Andrew Leber is a graduate student at Harvard University's Department of Government. He has previously translated Sudanese, Syrian, Palestinian, and Iraqi literature, including 'It's Not Important, You're From There' by Arthur Yak Gabro in

The Book of Khartoum, 'The Worker' by Basra author Diaa Jubaili in *Iraq + 100*, and several works of poetry by Palestinian poet Dareen Tatour.

Yasmine Seale is working on a new translation of the *Thousand and One Nights* for W. W. Norton. She lives in Istanbul.

Adam Talib is the translator of Fadi Azzam's *Sarmada*, Khairy Shalaby's *The Hashish Waiter*, and Mekkawi Said's *Cairo Swan Song*. With Katharine Halls, he co-translated Raja Alem's *The Dove's Necklace*. Other translations include Ahmed al-Malik's 'The Tank' in *The Book of Khartoum* (2015), Abdallah Tayeh's 'Two Men' in *The Book of Gaza* (2014), and Khaled Kaki's 'Operation Daniel' in *Iraq + 100* (2016). He teaches classical Arabic literature at the American University in Cairo.

ALSO AVAILABLE IN THE 'READING THE CITY' SERIES...

The Book of Khartoum

Edited by Raph Cormack & Max Shmookler

'An exciting, long-awaited collection showcasing
some of Sudan's finest writers.' – *Leila Aboulela*

Khartoum, according to one theory, takes its name from the Beja
word *hartooma*, meaning 'meeting place'. Geographically, culturally
and historically, the Sudanese capital is certainly that: a meeting place
of the Blue and White Niles, a confluence of Arabic and African
histories, and a destination point for countless refugees displaced by
Sudan's long, troubled history of forced migration.

In the pages of this book, the city also stands as a meeting place for
ideas: where the promise and glamour of the big city meets its tough
social realities; where traces of a colonial past are still visible in day-
to-day life; where the dreams of a young boy, playing in his father's
shop, act out a future that may one day be his. Diverse literary styles
also come together here: the political satire of Ahmed al-Malik; the
surrealist poetics of Bushra al-Fadil; the social realism of the first
postcolonial authors; and the lyrical abstraction of the new 'Iksir'
generation. As with any great city, it is from these complex tensions
that the best stories begin.

*Featuring: Bushra al-Fadil, Isa al-Hilu, Ali al-Makk, Ahmed al-Malik,
Bawadir Bashir, Mamoun Eltlib, Rania Mamoun, Abdel Aziz Baraka
Sakin, Arthur Gabriel Yak & Hammour Ziada.*

ISBN: 978-1-90558-372-0
£9.99

The Book of Tehran

Edited by Fereshteh Ahmadi

'A beautiful, insightful peek into a lesser-explored
area of the world and its literature.' – *Storgy*

A city of stories – short, fragmented, amorphous, and at times
contradictory – Tehran is an impossible tale to tell. For the capital city
of one of the most powerful nations in the Middle East, its literary
output is rarely acknowledged in the West. This unique celebration of
its writing brings together ten stories exploring the tensions and
pressures that make the city what it is: tensions between the public
and the private, pressures from without – judgemental neighbours,
the expectations of religion and society – and from within – family
feuds, thwarted ambitions, destructive relationships. The psychological
impact of these pressures manifests in different ways: a man wakes up
to find a stranger relaxing in his living room and starts to wonder if
this is his house at all; a struggling writer decides only when his
girlfriend breaks his heart will his work have depth... In all cases,
coping with these pressures leads us, the readers, into an unexpected
trove of cultural treasures – like the burglar, in one story, descending
into the basement of a mysterious antique collector's house –
treasures of which we, in the West, are almost wholly ignorant.

*Featuring: Fereshteh Ahmadi, Atoosa Afshin-Navid, Kourosh Asadi,
Azardokht Bahrami, Hamed Habibi, Mohammad Hosseini, Amirhossein
Khorshidfar, Payam Nasser, Goli Taraghi & Mohammad Tolouei*

ISBN: 978-1-91097-424-7
£9.99

Iraq + 100

Edited by Hassan Blasim

'Compelling, mind-expanding fiction'
– *Guy Gunaratne*

Iraq + 100 poses a question to ten Iraqi writers: what might your country look like in the year 2103 – a century after the disastrous American- and British-led invasion, and 87 years down the line from its current, nightmarish battle for survival? How might the effects of that one intervention reach across a century of repercussions, and shape the lives of ordinary Iraqi citizens, or influence its economy, culture, or politics? Might Iraq have finally escaped the cycle of invasion and violence triggered by 2003 and, if so, what would a new, free Iraq look like?

Covering a range of approaches – from science fiction, to allegory, to magic realism – these stories use the blank canvas of the future to explore the nation's hopes and fears in equal measure. Along the way a new aesthetic for the 'Iraqi fantastical' begins to emerge: thus we meet time-travelling angels, technophobic dictators, talking statues, macabre museum-worlds, even hovering tiger-droids, and all the time buoyed by a dark, inventive humour that, in itself, offers hope.

Featuring: Anoud, Hassan Abdulrazzak, Ibrahim Al-Marashi, Zhraa Alhaboby, Ali Bader, Hassan Blasim, Mortada Gzar, Jalal Hasan, Diaa Jubaili & Khalid Kaki

ISBN: 978-1-90558-366-9
£9.99

Thirteen Months of Sunrise

Rania Mamoun

'A phenomenal, exacting collection'
- Preti Taneja

A young woman sits by her father's deathbed, lamenting her failure to keep a promise to him...

A struggling writer walks every inch of the city in search of inspiration, only to find it is much closer than she imagined...

A girl collapses from hunger at the side of the road and is rescued by the most unlikely of saviours...

In this powerful, debut collection of stories, Rania Mamoun expertly blends the real and imagined to create a rich, complex and moving portrait of contemporary Sudan. From painful encounters with loved ones to unexpected new friendships, Mamoun illuminates the breadth of human experience and explores, with humour and compassion, the alienation, isolation and estrangement that is urban life.

'A stunning collection, remarkable for its sweet clarity of voice and startling depictions of the marginalised and the destitute. With mastery, Rania Mamoun reaches straight into the heartbeat of her subject matter, laying bare humanity in all its tenderness and tenacity.'
– Leila Aboulela, author of *Elsewhere Home*

Translated from the Arabic by Elisabeth Jaquette.

ISBN: 978-1-91097-439-1
£9.99